CW00557314

SINGLE DAD MATCHMATE

JADE ALTERS

© Copyright 2020 - Untamed Love, LLC - All rights reserved.

It is not legal to reproduce, duplicate, or transmit any part of this document in either electronic means or in printed format. Recording of this publication is strictly prohibited and any storage of this document is not allowed unless with written permission from the publisher except for the use of brief quotations in a book review.

This book is a work of fiction. Any resemblance to persons, living or dead, or places, events or locations is purely coincidental.

A NOTE FROM JADE

Have you joined my exclusive readers list? Be the first to hear about new releases, promotions and giveaways!

[Yes. Sign me up, please!]

Follow me on Facebook

JadeAlters.com

VICTORIA

$\mathcal{H}$ow many times would I tolerate a man answering his phone during a date? One? Two? How about six?

I swirled my glass before taking a sip. At least the merlot was good. The interruptions might have been excusable if my date was a surgeon. Or a therapist. Or even a professor, counseling students near finals.

But this man wasn't any of those things. He was a financial advisor, perpetually on the hunt for new clients. As a business owner myself, I understood the urge. But this had become excessive.

Now off the phone, he grinned at me through a mouthful of kale salad. "I see one of my clients over there. I'm going to go say hello."

I stabbed my fork into a piece of Tuscan-Style roasted asparagus. If I didn't have my reputation to consider, I'd walk out now.

Unbelievable. My so-called date led his client back over to our table. "Victoria, I'd like you to meet the owner of—" I tuned him out as he droned on, but I managed to refrain from crossing my arms. I smiled in the right places and offered my hand.

This date was a dud. He was another dull, pale-faced, self-obsessed businessman wearing a tailored suit. If he could stare lovingly at his phone on a date, so could I.

I sent a quick text to the newest number I'd saved in my phone: *I'm ready. I need your first available appointment. ASAP!*

Located in Midtown Manhattan, the agency was not what I expected. The inside of the office looked like a residence. The owner came out to meet me immediately and pushed a mimosa into my hand.

She caught me staring at the couches and dining table. "We didn't want Victory Matchmaking to feel like an office. We wanted it to feel like a home," she said. For the $25,000 fee, I figured she was right.

She ushered me to a sofa. "Tell me about what you want. None of this will leave the room. I'll make notes, but I'll write them as my interpretations."

The citrus was bitter on my tongue as I swallowed. "I don't know how to say what I want without sounding like a judgmental harpy."

She leaned in toward me. "You are here to get what you want."

How shallow was I going to sound when I admitted the truth of what I was looking for? "I know it's not PC, but I want an Alpha man. I don't mean one that dominates in the boardroom. I mean one that can throw a punch and shoot a gun."

She scribbled some notes. "I'm getting the picture. Tell me more."

"I want someone taller than me. I want a man who can

chop wood, and hammer a nail. I don't want him to be a selfish jerk, but I want to be able to tell the difference between him and my friends." I rubbed my hand over my face. "God, speaking of friends, they would be mortified to hear me saying these things."

She leaned in even closer. "I'd bet some of them secretly want the same thing."

"No." I had watched them over the years. I wasn't like them, not at all. "They want workaholic doctors, lawyers, and accountants. They want their husbands to pay for vacations, nannies, and private school." I sighed and dropped my head back on the sofa. "I fund my own life. I don't need a man to do it for me." I straightened back up. This was no time to lounge around. "I want a partner that I feel passion for. You'd think I could find him myself in a place like New York City."

"People hire you because you're an expert in web design and media. Let me be the expert in this." She gave me a firm tap on the knee. "I can find the right man for you," she assured me.

I picked up my pen. "Show me where to sign," I said. If she could find me the right match, this would be worth every penny. I was done wasting my time with losers.

LUKE

The flames were out, but thick smoke billowed in front of me. I held on tight to the woman I carried over my shoulder. Just a few more steps, and we'd be outside. Ten steps later, I staggered into the fresh air, sagging with relief as the paramedics took her from me.

I groaned as I leaned my head against my SUV and took a deep breath. But just one, because I had to get my kids to a birthday party. Which was the very last thing I wanted to do after working for ten hours.

My real job was serving as the Sheriff of Pine River, but I also worked as a volunteer firefighter, along with a good portion of the rest of my family. Today an electrical fire had trapped two employees in a storage closet at the hardware store. They were safe, thank God, but it was close.

I thought about resigning at least twice a day. But the fire department needed me—most employees were replaceable, but a shifter firefighter wasn't. As shifters, we could move faster and lift more than the average person. If I could respond to a call, it might save a human. A human who was

4

my kids' teacher, doctor, or friend. How could I say no to that?

After a short drive, I was finally home, or close to it. I stopped by my sister's house to collect the kids. "Daddy!" my kids screeched as they piled on top of me. "It's time for the party!" My daughter Beth yelled at the top of her lungs.

"They ate lunch," my sister Jane said. "We had pork chops and mashed potatoes."

I hugged her tightly. "Thank you. One day I'll repay you for this."

"Nah. I like it that you owe me." She punched me in the arm. "You know we're all in this together."

That was one benefit of the bear clan. We all lived on the same street, and we all had each other's backs, rain or shine, whether we enjoyed it or not.

And I hated to admit it, but I did need their help. My hours as sheriff were always uncertain. I'd officially retired from my first career as a soldier in special forces, made up only of shifters, but a few times a year the Army called me back to help my MASK.

I missed my MASK unit. But the travel was non-stop, and I had the kids now. The job came with some significant risks, and the kids were already down one parent—they didn't need to lose the only one they had left because I couldn't let go.

"Let's go guys, we've got to hurry." I grabbed a kid under each arm and hauled ass to the party, which was to celebrate my daughter's friend turning seven. In the birthday kid's backyard, every single thing was pirate-themed. The hostess was handing out eye patches for everyone, even the adults. It was a fucking madhouse.

Sure I had extra stamina as a shifter, but I was beat. I bowed out of socializing and slept in the car for two hours. After it was over, Beth bounced into the car. "Dad! Do you think we can have a mom?" she asked as she buckled her seat belt.

"Yeah!" Adam added as I helped him with his booster seat. "Moms make stuff like that. Tony said his mom's making a monster truck themed party!"

What the hell? He was five, and he knew about party themes? I didn't even remember being five.

Another unanticipated consequence of single-parenting —I sucked at crafts or whatever this would be classified as. I wasn't sexist enough to think it automatically fell to the mom. But they did seem to be the ones that made the fun stuff happen. I'd managed exactly one party for the kids. We'd only invited family, but even with cousins, we'd had fifteen kids. I'd texted them to be at the local pool at 2 p.m. and I'd shown up with a cake. I felt like I did a damn good job.

"Guys, moms aren't just for doing stuff that you want," I said. I backed the car up and started the path back home. "Moms are just like dads. Their job is to love you and take care of you."

"Yeah, like Aunt Jane!" My son chimed in. "Except Aunt Jane wrapped all of our presents to look like snowmen at Christmas."

I stared at Adam's hopeful face in the rearview mirror. On Christmas Eve, I had gotten off a double shift. I'd stuffed every gift inside bags. My mom and sisters would have been happy to take over and come wrap my presents, but I already depended on them so much. I wanted to be able to handle our family on my own, as much as I could.

"You guys really want a mom around? For real?" I thought kids didn't want their parents to date? Maybe that would be true if they had a mom they saw half the time. Instead, thanks to the nutcase I'd mated with, they had no mother at all.

"Yes!" They shouted in unison.

"What if she makes you eat broccoli every day? What then?"

"You make us eat it, Daddy!" Adam said.

Not very successfully. "Hmmm. What if she makes you clean the toilets with your hands?" I asked as I pulled into our driveway.

"She wouldn't!" Beth pounded the back of my seat. "It's not like *Cinderella*, Daddy! You would pick a nice lady!"

I didn't do such a great job the first go around. I promised myself I wouldn't bash my ex to the kids, no matter how tempting. When I was with my family or friends, all bets were off. If I had a few beers in close succession, I called her some pretty creative names.

I opened the door to the backseat to let the kids out. "She might! What if... she tickles you all day, like this?" I grabbed each kid and flipped them upside down. I was done discussing my love life with my kids.

By 9 p.m. the kids were asleep, and I was alone. No one to talk to, no one to watch TV with, and no one to sleep with. I didn't miss my ex, not really. She sucked for leaving her kids —there was no way to sugarcoat what she'd done. But I did miss having another adult in the house.

Maybe dating wouldn't be such a bad idea.

The next day the entire family got together to swim at the lake. I dumped a few dozen hot dogs onto the grill. "The kids want a mom," I said to my mother.

"They're right." My mom tapped me on the chest. "Those cubs do need a mom."

I looked over at my kids where they were digging in the sandy dirt with their cousins. "I thought I was doing fine."

"Luke Thomas. You know that is not what I meant," my mom scolded. "A grandmother and two aunts are not the same as a mother, no matter how invested they are." My mom's eyes widened. She clapped her hands together. "I know just the person."

Oh good Lord. Why had I told my mother? The air was cool enough, but between the heat from the grill and my mother's meddling, my temperature was about a thousand degrees. "Mom, please don't set me up on any dates. I don't want it to get awkward." Like the time one of the preschool teachers was interested. Or the mom of one of Beth's friends. Or one of the female firefighters.

My mom added a few more hot dogs to the grill. She never thought we had enough food. To her credit, feeding a sleuth of bear shifters was not an easy task.

"I'm not setting you up on a date," she said, squeezing my arms. "There's a professional matchmaker in Fayetteville. I just saw it on the news! And I know her."

I rammed a fork through one of the hot dogs at the edge of the grill. "A professional matchmaker?" I wiped the sweat from my forehead. "What the hell—is there a degree for that now?"

"She has a degree in sociology and psychology, and a master's in social work. She understands human behavior."

A breeze drifted by, but it did nothing to help me cool my heated skin. "I'm not human."

"Well any woman you meet most likely will be."

"If you think I need therapy, just say so." I wasn't opposed to that. I'd gone after a few brutal missions when I was working with my MASK unit.

"Would you please listen? She's not a therapist. She matches you with a compatible woman. It's much more reliable than a blind date."

I scooped all the hot dogs off the grill. I had to get away

from my mom before she had a wedding planned for a non-existent wife.

"If you found someone, she could help with the kids," my sister said, laying her chin on top of my shoulder.

I jumped into the air. "Where did you come from? Were you eavesdropping?" I whacked my sister with a spatula. "And that is not why I'd date."

My sister stuck a piece of cheese in her mouth. "Just sayin'."

It sounded like a fucking nightmare.

"Give it a try. What could it hurt?" Jane said.

It could hurt a whole lot.

I hadn't exactly agreed to see the matchmaker. In fact, I gave my mother a very definite no.

But my mother, sister, and sister-in-law all showed up on Tuesday morning, beaming. They promised my kids a trip to the park, ice cream, and roller skating. So on my only day off, I drove to Fayetteville to pay someone to find me a date. Just how I wanted to spend my free time.

I did consider the fact that if I got remarried, it would probably make my family's life easier. They'd feel less pressure to make sure the kids had a female presence. They tried to fill in for my ex—they showed up for class parties, fundraisers, and soccer practices. I was present as often as possible, but as sheriff, I was constantly getting called away.

How pathetic was it to have to pay for a date? This matchmaker would probably think I couldn't get one on my own, whereas the opposite was true. I knew it sounded arrogant, but quite a few women had pursued me since my ex bailed. This wasn't my own opinion, but I'd had at least six women tell me I was a catch, simply because I wasn't afraid of commitment, I was hard-working, and I liked kids.

I could not believe I was doing this.

Buck up. It's for your kids. You walk into burning buildings. You've run covert operations in deadly locations. You can face a matchmaker.

The matchmaker already had the door open when I got out of my car. "You must be Luke!" Her smile was wide. "I was so excited to hear from your mother."

Here goes nothing.

VICTORIA

"*I* have found the perfect man for you," the matchmaker said as she peered at me over her glasses. "However, I don't want you to immediately discount him because of his location."

Another day, another mimosa at Victory Matchmaking. This one was sweeter rather than bitter. "Now I'm curious."

"He's in Arkansas," she said, speaking quickly. "If you'll give it a chance, then--"

I held up my hand. I didn't need someone to convince me the south could be a decent place to live. "I'm from south Arkansas. My grandmother lived in Fayetteville. I spent a lot of time there growing up."

She adjusted her glasses and blinked at me a few times. "You're from Arkansas? I had no idea."

"No one does." At least she was too professional to make the usual jokes about me having all my teeth and wearing shoes. And she didn't comment on my lack of accent. I didn't work to drop my southern twang because I was ashamed. I dropped it because I wanted clients to focus on my work, and not the way I talked.

She handed over a sealed folder. "He's thirty-four. He's a former military officer. He's currently the elected sheriff in Pine River, a volunteer firefighter and he has two children, ages five and six. His ex-wife has no contact. He does have a lot of extended family living in the area, and he owns his home."

She stopped short of actually telling me his name. She explained the agency prefers to remove the temptation for clients to internet stalk their dates before meeting them. They find it makes the clients more receptive to their matches. Although it irked me slightly, I understood sometimes too much information can be a bad thing.

It sounded like she'd made this guy up for me. I was a little nervous about the kids, but not opposed. "When do I meet him?"

"As soon as you're ready. The agency will set up a plane ticket and hotel for you." She kept talking, explaining the process for the first date, but I couldn't focus. My mind skipped ahead. I didn't want to fly down to Arkansas, spend the weekend with a guy, and then come back to the city. I wanted a change in my life.

A very big change. "You know what? Go ahead and make the arrangements. But don't get me a return ticket. This is going to sound crazy, but I'm going to go stay in Arkansas for a while. I could use a break from the city. I'm going to give this a shot."

Her eyebrows shot up. "Ah. Okay. I didn't expect that. But we will certainly do whatever we can to accommodate you."

Thank goodness this was confidential. I would not be telling anyone else I was moving, however temporarily, to another state to go on a date with a man I'd never met.

Because that was one-hundred percent crazy.

If any friend of mine told me she was moving for a blind

date, I'd stage an intervention. I'd call her family, her friends, her co-workers—anyone I could think of to make her stop.

But Luke was only a small portion of my motivation. When I moved to New York City, I'd loved everything it had to offer. I took nothing for granted. Not the theater, or the museums, or the opportunities. But the life I lived now was nothing like that. I worked, and I went out.

I was sick of the social engineering. Of the jockeying for party invites. I didn't want any more dinner parties or weekends in the Hamptons or ferry rides to Nantucket. I didn't want to attend a gala, or sit on a board.

I wanted a normal life, like the one I had growing up. I wanted a family, with kids that I drove to school each day. I didn't want my future kids on a waiting list—since birth—for a Kindergarten where the moms wanted to one-up each other. I wanted to come home to a house with a swing set, and I wanted to go for a bike ride, or to a movie on a date night with the father of my children.

New York City could be a great place to raise a kid, if that's what you wanted. But I needed a break. That evening, it struck me as I packed my bags that I had nothing to care for here. No pets. No plants. No partner. No children. I'd hired the right people to run my company while I was away, and it really was time to go.

I might not have anyone depending on me directly, but I did owe Aria a phone call. My Director of Operations kept me on track when my left brain overpowered my right, and I locked myself away creating designs, instead of managing a company. She kept an eye on every department, and brought some of my pie-in-the-sky ideas back down to earth. Without her, our profits wouldn't be nearly so high.

"What's up, boss?" she said over the speaker.

"Hi, Aria. I'm going out of town for a while."

"The conference in Paris isn't until August. Wait." There was a loud scuffling sound as she picked up the phone. "Are you going on vacation? I'm going to forbid you from taking your laptop. You know we have it covered."

"It's a working vacation. I'm going home to Arkansas for a while."

"But your parents are in Canada."

"Yes. I saw them last month."

"So…"

"Are you trying to ask me why I'd willingly visit Arkansas?"

"I didn't say that…"

I laughed. "Arkansas is wonderful. The landscapes are breathtaking, the people are nice, and there are very few crowds anywhere."

We chatted for a few more minutes about specific projects we had open, and then we said goodbye. I was in a daze on the way to the airport, and while waiting to board. I couldn't believe I was about to leave the state for a man. But I wasn't turning back now.

I cleaned out my inbox and left an out-of-office message on my email and voicemail, but I checked my email one last time before the plane took off.

There was one email, from my CFO. She usually stuck to our office Slack program for sending me messages. Maybe Slack was down. I'd go ahead and read it before I was unavailable for a few hours.

Hi Victoria,

I've attached the notes from our strategy meeting, i.e. expanding our non-profit charity scholarship program. Let me know what you think.

We just met yesterday to discuss expanding our scholarship program for girls who were interested in web development. I clicked on the attachment, eager to see the summary of our meeting, and any other ideas she'd had. Odd. It wasn't the notes from the strategy meeting. It was an article—a lovely write up highlighting the rapid growth of our company, with details about our recent expansion.

She must have attached the wrong document, which wasn't like her at all. I'd have to ask her about it later.

For now, I had three hours to relax and drop my NYC mindset before embarking on this new adventure.

In Pine River, I found a charming restaurant called Apple Pie Diner. Or it was lovely until it caught on fire. Right as I bit into their spicy chicken sandwich, I smelled smoke.

A second later, two waiters shoved the doors open. "Get outside! Go! Run!" they screamed.

I didn't run, but I did go to the patio. Above the roof, a thin line of gray smoke hovered in the air.

A truck yanked to a stop in front of the building, and a man wearing full firefighting gear, minus the helmet, jumped out of the truck. He was stunning, even with the thick gear on. His brown hair was full, his jaw was strong, and his skin was a pretty tan, with just a little scruff on his face. My eyes met his as he pushed his way into the building. He was back out soon after, but this time he grabbed a ladder from his truck.

A few minutes later, an ambulance arrived, along with a car that said sheriff on it. The men and women that raced inside were all fit and gorgeous, though not one compared to the first firefighter.

Eventually, that first firefighter appeared. He raked his hand through his thick brown hair. A little soot was streaked across his handsome face but it only added to his looks. If this was how the men were made in Pine River, then my move to Arkansas was worth it, even if I only looked and never got to touch.

LUKE

Friday afternoon usually meant taking the kids to get pizza and then renting a movie. This Friday afternoon, I had a date.

My ex and I hadn't dated. I'd known her since we were kids, and we were both shifters. We fell into the relationship because we were hot for each other, and I never really asked her out. Now at thirty-four years old, I was facing a blind date.

I'd had it all planned out: I left work early. I arranged to have one of the deputies take over for me, but right as I pulled into my driveway, my phone rang.

Dammit. It was one of the waiters at the Apple Pie Diner. They knew calling me was the fastest way to get help, and they needed it—the owner had tried to put the fire out himself, and managed to break his arm in the process. Now the fire had snaked up the wall, singed the plaster and scorched the ceiling. I grabbed my gear and ran. I didn't want to screw up my date, but I couldn't let the owner get hurt.

As a first responder, I got the fire out with a heavy-duty fire blanket and a fire extinguisher. I got the owner's arm splinted, and made sure the paramedics were on the way. A frantic thirty minutes after I arrived, I was no longer needed. I checked on all the staff inside, then headed to the outside dining area to check on the staff there.

Outside the diner, a woman stood on the patio, apart from the staff. She'd caught my eye on the way in, because she was so striking that she looked out of place.

Now that I had the time, I studied her a little closer as I chatted with the staff, who all seemed to be fine. I hoped I wasn't being creepy. The people in Pine River weren't poor, but I wouldn't say any of them were particularly fancy. But this woman was refined in a way I hadn't often seen, even out of Arkansas.

Her posture was straight and her shoulders were pulled back. Even after the mad scramble of evacuating from the diner, her sleek haircut was perfectly in place. The sun is shining right in her face and the situation hadn't messed up her polished makeup. She wore fitted pants and a pristine white button-down blouse. She must be a tourist, although usually the tourists were dressed for hiking or camping.

I couldn't stop staring at her. I'd seen women like her in movies, but never here.

My bear rumbled. He liked her too. He wished she was our date tonight.

Shut it. You couldn't keep your hands off your ex, and look how well that worked out.

I tore my eyes away. I either needed to say hello, or get the hell away from her. I pulled my heavy gloves off and slung my fire coat over my arm. I was the sheriff, and self-appointed welcoming committee. I always greeted new residents. Not that we got many.

I wasn't leaving here without saying hello. Then I could put her out of my mind for good. There was no way a simple guy like me could keep up with a woman that looked like that.

I tugged my helmet off, knowing my hair would be wild. But wild hair was better than a dorky helmet. "Hello ma'am," I said.

VICTORIA

I shaded my eyes. I blinked up at the sexy firefighter towering over me. He'd just said hello to me, and called me ma'am. No one had ever called me ma'am in New York. But as a child in Arkansas, everyone had been ma'am. And in his deep baritone, it was nothing but sexy.

He'd come blazing in, saved the owner, the building, and then checked on all the staff. I'd never seen anything like it, at least not in person. The men I'd dated hired help for any physical task, whether it was cleaning, cooking, or lawn care.

He wore only a black t-shirt, with his jacket draped over his arm. I couldn't stop my eyes from traveling over the shirt where it stretched across his chest and over his biceps.

The flush flowed over my entire body. *Now, why did you leave Arkansas again? You never saw a man like this in the city.*

"Hello," I stammered, trying to recover my cool. I pointed to the smoldering roof. "Does this happen often?"

"Often enough." He gave me a crooked grin. "We don't have a real fire department here, so residents get creative.

They feel bad if we have to come out a lot, so the owner here tried to handle a kitchen fire himself." He shook his head. "I wish they wouldn't. I'm just glad it wasn't worse."

"Are you a volunteer?" My dad had been a rural volunteer firefighter when I was a kid. The men I dated in the city made plenty of charitable donations, but always for tax write-offs, or networking opportunities. They only volunteered their time if they gained something tangible in return.

"I am. Volunteer firefighter, not a volunteer sheriff." His grin grew wider and his deep green eyes sparkled. "My name's Luke Thomas."

He was exactly the kind of man I wanted. He brave, he risked his life to help others, and he wasn't even paid to do it. Suddenly something clicked - he sounded exactly like the guy the matchmaker set me up with... could it be?! What are the chances this small town has two guy's that fit my blind date's description? But what can I say really? *Hey, are you perhaps going on a blind date that you severely overpaid for later?*

What are the chances that I'd run into my match the moment I arrive in town though? Doubts start to creep in. There's no way the matchmaker could possibly have landed me the perfect man on the first go-round.

He was probably married. I glanced at his left hand. No wedding ring. But that didn't mean much if he was working. I couldn't imagine any little town like this would let him stay single long.

I held out my hand and smiled. "I'm Victoria Brantley."

"I don't know if you want me to shake your hand." He nodded at the gloves he held. "Even before I had the gloves on I was helping someone get their goats back in the fence."

My smile hurt my face now. I had to tone it down. "I don't mind at all."

He shrugged. "Fine by me."

His hand, large and warm, covered mine.

I gave my best firm handshake, trying to keep it professional. This was the town sheriff, and probably the most competent firefighter as well. I couldn't look like a mindless twit, smitten over the first real man I've seen in too long.

But that's exactly what I was.

"Are you visiting Pine River, Miss Brantley?"

My city friends would have wrinkled their noses at the "Miss." But I liked it. It was familiar to me.

"I'm going to be staying for a while. I was living in New York, and I needed a break." That was true enough. "I lived in Arkansas as a child."

"We don't get many new people here. What part of town are you staying in, if you don't mind me asking?"

I did not mind him asking, not one bit. In the city, I'd never have given a stranger a hint of where I lived. But surely this guy was safe. He was the sheriff after all. "I'm renting a cottage on Hickory Street."

"Oh, that's a great neighborhood. Not far from where I live."

I had to restrain myself from giving him the exact address. What had come over me? Is this what happened to me when I was attracted to someone for real? "I'm glad to hear it."

"I hope you like it." He inclined his head towards me. "Nice to meet you. If you need anything, let me know."

My stomach fluttered. I didn't often have such carnal thoughts, but I wanted to rip his clothes off. I pressed my lips together. I had to get it together before I made a spectacle of myself.

Our conversation was the simplest I'd ever had, yet I wanted more.

"I'll do that. Thank you for the welcome." I picked up my bag. As much as I wanted to spend more time with him, I had a date. "It was so nice to meet you." If the other men in this town were anything like Luke, then I'd made the right decision to come stay for a while.

"I'll see you around I'm sure," he said.

I certainly hoped so.

LUKE

I did not want to leave Victoria. I stood there like a dope while she waved goodbye. Even her wave was graceful.

I watched her walk away. In those snug jeans, every sway of her hips showed off her cute little backside.

My bear wanted to chase her.

Not okay, dude. I'm on duty. Plus we don't chase humans.

I had to get ready for my date. I hurried home, wrestled with the kids for a few minutes and dropped them off with my sister.

I didn't have "date" clothes. I put on a clean pair of jeans and a new button-down shirt my mom had forced on me— with great glee—when she heard about the date.

We were meeting at a restaurant in Fayetteville, as the dating service recommended. I didn't know any details, other than I needed to be there at 8 p.m. for our reservation. More than once, I considered canceling the date and finding Victoria. I must have been out of my mind to agree to meet a stranger.

I walked into the restaurant, and there, seated under a

window was Victoria. My skin tingled all over, just from seeing her again. What were the odds that she was here too? Realistically, it wasn't that crazy—this was the most popular date place in Fayetteville. But watching her have dinner with a date of her own was going to drive me nuts.

"I'm meeting someone," I told the hostess, my eyes still glued to Victoria. "Table twenty." The hostess nodded as she check her tablet. I'm sure it had a big red PAID FOR A DATE written next to my name.

Oh well. I'd survived worse things than a hostess knowing I used a dating service. Supposedly all the cloak and dagger stuff where we met at a designated place was to keep the participants safe. After what I'd seen in the military, and as a sheriff, I couldn't say it was a bad idea.

"Right this way sir." The hostess led me straight to Victoria.

Victoria Brantley was my date.

My bear settled down as he saw her. I hadn't even noticed he'd been restless. But now a contented weight rolled over me, calming the tingling skin I'd had when I walked in. *Mine.*

Slow down, buddy.

Victoria gave me a pleased smile. "Fancy meeting you here." She laughed. "I've always wanted to say that."

I pulled my chair out and sat down. "You're my date. That's awesome." I couldn't exactly make a cutting remark about needing help with a date if Victoria was in the same boat. "I'm glad it's you. When we met earlier, I was really hoping it would be you but I couldn't be sure."

"Well when we met earlier, I considered canceling my date," I replied softly. *God, I hope I'm not being too forward.* It's been a long time since I'd been on a date.

She smoothed her hand over her already perfect hair. "But you're too much of a gentleman to cancel for no reason."

I glanced down and spotted my napkin. I unfolded and

stuck it on my lap, thanks to my sister's countless reminders to not act like an actual animal. "I don't know that anyone has called me a gentleman. Ever."

Her pink lips formed a cute bow. "I don't believe it." Tonight she wore a yellow sundress that looked great with her dark hair. Her bare arms were toned, but slender. I wanted to touch them, but I kept my hands to myself.

"I'll demonstrate," I said. "Because I'm going to ask you right now if you've ever done this before."

Her eyes twinkled. "Done what? Gone on a date?" She picked up her glass of red wine and took a sip. "Eaten at a restaurant?"

Oh, she was fun. I'd been asked out plenty of times, but it had been a while since any of the women in town flirted with me. "I bet I know the answer to both of those." I pointed at her. "You know what I mean."

She folded her arms over and leaned in closer to me. "You mean have I been *so* pathetic that I had to hire a service to find someone to go out with me?"

I laughed. "I hardly think I can throw stones."

"Yes." She sat back up straight as a waiter approached. "It was my first time using a dating service. You?"

"Same," I said as the waiter stepped up to ask us what we wanted to eat. We ordered, ate and never stopped talking.

By 10 p.m., we were still talking, but our glasses hadn't been refilled, and I'd paid for our meal long ago. The waiter had began to give us disapproving stares. "I think they're ready for us to get out of here," I fake-whispered. "If we were in Pine River, they'd have just hit us with the brooms until we left."

She grinned. "I'd forgotten what this was like. You can lose track of time in the city that never sleeps."

I wasn't ready for our date to be over, but there was no way I was going to ask her back to my place, not yet. I wasn't going to risk offending her. I pushed my chair back and held out my hand to her.

She placed her small hand in mine as we wove our way out in between tables. "So you really left New York City to come back to Arkansas?" I asked as we stepped into the warm night air.

"Yes." Her fingers tightened in mine. "I didn't realize I'd missed it so much until I got back here." She lingered on the steps of the restaurant, making no move to get back to her car.

She's not ready for it to end either.

"Want to take a walk?" I asked. I had now become one giant dad cliche, suggesting after-dinner walks, but I didn't care. I wanted to spend time with her. I'd have preferred the Ozark Forest, but I got how utterly weird that would be to suggest for a first date.

"I'd love to," she said. We strolled through downtown Fayetteville, peering in store windows, and admiring the freshly blooming flowers. It was quieter than usual; many of the college students had gone home after their spring finals.

"What did you do in New York?" I asked her.

"I own a web design firm. I'm able to run it from here."

Impressive. "That sounds intense. You don't think you'll get bored down here? I've been to New York. There's a lot going on."

"I don't imagine I'll miss it at all. There's a lot going on down here too." She wiggled her fingers against my palm. That tiny touch sent sparks up my arm.

I had to clench my left hand into a fist to stave off the overpowering arousal that surged through my body. I wanted to press her up against a storefront door and cover her mouth with mine.

I blew out a breath. Deep breathing was not working— she smelled too good for it to calm me down. Luckily she asked me a few mundane questions about my job and my time in the military. After that, she asked me to tell her about my kids, which I was happy to do, but it cut off my arousal quickly.

I pulled my hand from hers and wrapped my arm around her slight shoulders. She took a step closer, fitting herself against my side.

She glanced up at me. "This is going to sound really rude," she said. "I know we joked about it earlier. But I have to ask. Why did you use an agency? I can't imagine you have any trouble finding dates."

I chuckled. "It's not rude. And I could ask you the same thing," I said.

"You first," she said.

Each time she tilted her head to look up at me, her sweet lavender smell sent waves of heat through my veins. I cleared my throat. This wasn't my favorite topic, but I was going to tell her the truth. "My ex, excuse my language, is a real piece of shit. She not only left me, she left the kids. She doesn't visit, she doesn't call, she doesn't write. I haven't been very eager to jump back into a relationship. Women have been interested, but it's not worth the trouble. Until now."

She stopped walking and turned to face me. "What changed?"

I couldn't very well tell her my kids wanted a mom. "My kids asked me to. They think it's weird that I'm alone. No one in our family is single. So here I am." I reached up and touched a strand of her hair. "Although if I'd met you today, I'd have asked you out."

I was spilling my guts to Victoria after knowing her for a few hours. No one had ever had that effect on me.

"I'm glad to hear that," she said. "I'm sorry about your ex." She put her hand on my arm. "I don't want to end our date, but I need to get up early for a cyber meeting tomorrow."

"It's ok. You're probably going to think I'm super over-bearing. But I'd normally take you home on a date. Can I follow you? These roads can be tricky if you're not used to driving on them."

"I'd like that." She raised on her tiptoes and pecked me on the cheek. "I told you that you were a gentleman."

I was still pretty far from one, but I wasn't going to argue with her again. I followed her on the twisting road to her house, and I walked her to the front door. "Thank you for a great evening," she said.

"I'd like to see you again, but my schedule is unpredictable," I said.

"I'm thirty years old. I can handle a postponed date. And I work from home. So if you're free on a random Wednesday morning, we can have breakfast."

"How do you feel about hiking?"

"I love it."

"Next Tuesday I'm off all day. Wanna hike in the Ozark Forest?" I hoped she liked hiking. It wasn't exactly a deal-breaker, but as mini-shifters who didn't yet shift, my kids were super active. I took them out as often as I could. If I did end up getting serious with Victoria, she'd have a lot of alone time while we're out on the lake, in the river, or the woods.

Our clan lived in Pine River because of its proximity to the forest, and once a week we met there to shift and hang out as bears, not that I'd be telling Victoria about that.

Although if I were to mate again, I'd have to tell the woman I was a shifter. That should be an interesting conversation.

I leaned in toward her, keeping my hands down, giving her plenty of time to move away, fully aware of my height and build compared to hers. She didn't back away. She moved closer, tilting her head back. I covered her lips with mine. Her mouth was sweet; she tasted like the butter pecan ice cream we'd shared at the restaurant.

My arousal was instant. I wanted to lift her, to carry her inside and take her to bed. But it was too soon. She had called me a gentleman twice. I was going to live up to that. I did lift her though, but instead of carrying her inside, I sat her on the porch railing. She didn't have to lean up to kiss me, and I put my hands on either side of her face. Her delicate cheeks were warm against my palms.

I licked into her mouth. She parted her legs and pulled at me, urging me to step between them. I pressed against her, taking her mouth, pushing my tongue inside. Her dress rode up, revealing her tan legs. Like her dress, her panties were yellow, and they pressed against the front of my jeans. She moaned and gripped my shoulders. If I was a human, I'd have no idea, but as a shifter, I could smell her arousal.

I put my hand on the outside of her knee. I slid my hand up over her bare thigh, stopping before I got to her panties. With one tug, I could have her stripped naked. With a few steps, I could have her in the bedroom, writhing under me.

No Luke. Stop. This is a first date.

I had to go, before I ripped the thin cotton of her sundress away.

I pulled back and leaned my forehead against a wooden post until I caught my breath. I moved back to her and kissed her forehead. "You are the sweetest thing I've ever tasted. But I'm going to let you get to bed."

She pressed her lips together. Her eyes were still glazed. I can't say I wasn't proud of that. I lifted her off the porch railing. I made sure her dress was back in place.

"Thank you for the date," I said. "I'll pick you up on Tuesday for the hike."

"I'll see you then, Mr. Thomas," she said. She turned to go inside, giving me one last grin over her shoulder.

I called my deputy to check-in, and to get my head back on straight before I went home. If every date with Victoria was like this, I might not survive.

Tuesday's date with Victoria was too far away.

Waiting sucked. I wanted to see her again, as soon as possible. My kids kept me busy over the weekend, but on Monday, I had a two-hour break during the workday. I texted Victoria: *How do you feel about kayaking?*

Twenty minutes later, I was in her driveway.

She came out dressed in a maroon t-shirt and crisp white shorts. The shorts showed off her shapely legs, which made me want to run my hands all over them. I pulled my eyes back up to her face. If I let my mind fixate on her body, I'd be stuck with a demanding physical reaction, and no way to take care of it.

Looking at her face wasn't much help. Her full lips were a rosy pink, and she'd pulled her glossy hair in a high ponytail that showed off her cheekbones.

Large sunglasses hid her green eyes, but her mouth curved into a smile.

"You look glamorous," I said.

Those rosy pink lips twisted up. "I'll take that as a compliment."

"I meant it as one." I bent down to kiss her cheek. She smelled amazing. I could place the scent now—she smelled like sugar and lavender. I had to stop myself from pressing my face to her neck and inhaling. For a shifter, it wouldn't be weird, but a human woman might not appreciate it.

She hopped in my truck and we bumped down the gravel road to the spot where we kayaked on the Pine River.

"The water is so clear," she said. "It reminds me of the

Buffalo River." She smiled up at me. "I'm relieved to see that it's gentle, and not white water."

"Have you been white water rafting?" I didn't want to tell her that with her delicate looks, I'd assumed she wasn't up for anything but flat water.

"I have. I went to Canada the last time. I've done a class III, with a tiny bit of class IV."

That was seriously impressive. Not only did she own her own company, she was adventurous too. The class IV river I'd tried had been fucking terrifying, and I was a lot harder to kill than the average human.

"Today will be a breeze for you, if you've handled white water." I handed her a lifejacket. "Sorry about the bulky flotation device. With me as sheriff, I can't get caught skipping the safety procedures."

She took it and held it against her chest. "Pretty fashionable. It's good that you follow the rules. I'd hate to have to report you, officer."

"Oh yeah? You'd turn me in?" I asked.

She pushed her glasses onto the top of her head. She looked at me with her bright green eyes. "That depends."

"On what?"

She put one hand on her hip. "You'll have to prove to me that you're a good citizen." She pursed her lips as she grinned at me. I could feel the heat coming off of her, and she was breathing harder than normal.

So much for avoiding the physical reaction. I was rock hard. I could suggest that we skip the kayaks, and go back to her place. But I had to get back to work, and so did she. I did not want to rush our first time together, but I had to kiss her again. I put my hand on the back of her neck and tilted her head back.

Her lifejacket hit the ground as her arms came up around me. Her lips were cool against mine. She might smell like sugar and lavender, but she tasted of strawberries and mint. I pulled her closer.

The slight weight of her body against mine had my senses on overload. The sounds of the river faded—all I could hear was the beat of her heart.

She stepped back, breaking our embrace. "People are coming," she said, turning her head to the right.

Damn. She was right. I'd been so wrapped up in her that I didn't even hear the noisy chatter of a group of college students coming right toward us.

"I guess we should stop," she said, letting go of me. My mind agreed, but my body did not. And neither did my bear. He wanted to carry her into the woods, far away from other people.

"Thanks. It's hard for me to lecture kids for excessive public displays of affection when I'm doing it too." Despite the loud group coming, my body was not getting the message that it was time to cool off. I waded into the river. It was eighty-five degrees outside, but the river water was frigid. I splashed some water on my face just in case.

Do not ask her if she wants to leave. This is not the time. You can wait.

The cold water did its job— until I stepped over to help her into the kayak. My hand brushed over her leg, and the feel of her smooth skin against mine sent my heart skyrocketing.

As soon as we were seated, she looked over at me and smiled. She pulled the lifejacket over her pert breasts and snapped the buckle closed.

It looked like I'd be paddling while turned on. It wasn't something I'd done before. But around Victoria, it might be a permanent state of existence.

VICTORIA

*Y*esterday Luke had taken me kayaking on his lunch break.

Today was his day off, and as promised, he took me to the Ozark National Forest.

Luke was still too good to be true. I was getting exactly what I wanted from dating him.

If I'd suggested an outdoor sport to any of the city guys I'd dated, they'd have run the other way.

The weather was warm, with just the slightest breeze, and the sun filtered in through the leaves overhead. Branches rustled as birds landed in the trees above us, chirping madly as we picked our way up a hill.

"Want to see the waterfall?" he asked, pointing to a trail right ahead of us. "It's uphill the whole way."

I crossed my arms. "Are you implying I can't make it?"

He laughed. "I didn't say that!"

I gave him a gentle smack on the arm. "I'll have you know I've done quite a bit of hiking. I hiked the Half Dome in Yosemite." It was years ago, but I didn't need to mention that.

"Well then. I guess you don't need my help."

"I didn't say that. But..." I tapped my foot against the rock. "We could race." I took off before he could protest. I couldn't beat him, but I thought it would be fun to try.

"You're going down," he said, but he stayed behind me until we reached part of the trail where the dirt turned into large stones, some lying sideways. Somehow, he popped in front of me. "I won," he said, standing upon a rock about five feet higher than the one I was on.

I looked behind me. "How in the world did you get up here?" I pointed to a boulder a few away. "You were just back there!"

He smirked. "Superior skill."

"We aren't to the waterfall yet!" I moved to take off again, but he grabbed my waist.

"Yeah, but you have to be careful here," he said. "This one's not stable at all." He demonstrated, showing how the boulder tipped back and forth as he shifted his weight.

I peered up at him. "We'll have a rematch later."

"I wouldn't miss it," he said. He held out his hand, and I placed my palm in his. He pulled me up, but he pulled so hard that I flew forward.

I stumbled and crashed into his chest.

"Sorry," he said, laughing as he caught me by the arms. "You're so tiny."

"I'm not tiny," I said. "You're just big." *And I love that you are.*

Was it shallow that his size was a constant turn on? His sculpted face was eye-catching. On our previous dates, women stopped to stare at him. But I stayed fixated on his height, his broad shoulders, and his firm muscles.

We were in the middle of a race, but I didn't step away from where I was plastered to his chest.

I looked up as his face.

Did I just bat my eyelashes at him? I'm already dating him, I don't have to make eyes at him.

One of the guys I'd dated called me The Ice Queen. I'd heard that sentiment before. Men had said I was cold, aloof, reserved. I didn't feel like any of those terms applied to me when I was with Luke. With Luke, I found myself doing things I'd scorned before.

I was aware of my body in a way I'd never been. I wanted Luke to look at me, to notice me. If a former boyfriend had admired me, it was flattering—sometimes. But it didn't turn me on. With Luke, it was arousing. The feeling was utterly bizarre, and yet intoxicating. I didn't just want him to look at me; I wanted him to like what he saw.

And that happened quite a bit. Yesterday while kayaking, I'd had a moment where I considered asking him to take me back home—to bed. I bit down on my tongue to stop myself. We hadn't even known each other a week. Now today, on our third date, I wasn't sure I'd have the same willpower.

I didn't want to rush into anything. But if he asked me, I would not be saying no. So far he'd initiated kissing me on both dates. Now it was my turn.

I might not have dated as much as some of my friends, but I could tell when a man wanted me, and Luke definitely did.

I tipped my head back. In the outside light, Luke's blue eyes were even brighter. His gaze was fixed on me. I could feel him taking measured breaths. He tipped his head closer to me. I wasn't wearing perfume today. I probably smelled like the woods, but Luke didn't seem to mind.

My hands rested on his strong biceps. My fingers flexed against his skin. "Nice view," I said.

He pulled me tighter against him. "You like it?"

"Yeah." I licked my lips. I'd eaten a mint just before we got out of the car. I hoped it was still effective. "I do like it." I looked down. Falling off a rock would not be sexy. My hiking boots didn't give me any extra height. I stepped on the next rock up. I wanted to be closer to Luke's face. I tightened my grip on his arms and leaned in. I pressed my mouth against his.

He stood completely still for a few seconds, except for the movement of his lips against mine. "I like these woods too. I like 'em even better now," he murmured.

His hands came to rest on the small of my back, and he tugged me closer. "Victoria," he breathed as he kissed me harder.

He groaned and dropped his arms to his sides. "I don't want to, but I have to stop. Anyone could walk up." He glanced down at the boulder we stood on. "Or we could fall right off this rock."

"It would be worth it," I said.

"Don't tempt me," he said. He took my hand. "Come on. Let's go back." We climbed back down the outcropping of rocks. He went in front of me, stepping sideways, and holding my hand over each slippery rock. As soon as we reached level ground, Luke tugged me off the path, behind a grouping of trees. He leaned against a tree trunk and pulled me against him. "No one's close by."

I didn't care if anyone was close by or not. I got as close to him as I could. I could feel his erection, hard against my hip. My stomach turned over. I wanted to unzip his pants. I wanted to touch him, to feel how much he wanted me. I settled for rocking my hips into his.

He groaned as he devoured my mouth. He lifted me, urging me to wrap my legs around his waist. He held me in the air easily.

My head spun. The fabric of my sports bra rubbed against my breasts as my nipples tightened.

"I can't have you here," he breathed. "But I want you. So much."

Right. Public indecency with the sheriff probably wasn't my best idea. "Let's go back to my place," I said.

He ducked down to look into my eyes. "You sure?"

"I'm positive." We'd waited long enough. I wanted Luke, and I was going to have him.

～

"You are." Luke stopped talking to kiss me as I pushed the door to my house open. "So beautiful."

I locked the door behind us. "It's been a long time for me," I said.

"You didn't date much in New York?"

"I did, but I didn't like anyone well enough to keep dating them."

"Lucky for me," he said, kissing down my neck.

I cringed away. I smelled like the outside. It was a pleasant enough smell, but I was probably sweaty overall. "Do you mind if I shower?"

Luke sniffed the air. "No. I could probably use one too." He kissed me again. "But you smell delicious."

"I'll be right back. If you'd like, you can use my second bathroom." I ran my hands over his wide shoulders. "I don't think I have anything you can wear."

He tugged at my tank top. "Yeah I think this might look like I'm wearing a washcloth," he said. "I keep extra clothes in my car. You never know what's going to happen when you're the sheriff."

"You get dirty? Were you chasing a suspect?"

"Every now and then. But the last time I was helping a farmer get his cows back inside the fence. Cow wrangling is part of my job description."

I was glad he wasn't in danger every day. "I'd like to see that, cowboy." "I'll be right back."

After scrubbing myself down, I wrung my hair out as much as I could. I pulled on a fresh sundress—Luke seemed to like the yellow one I wore on our first date. This one was white, and it showed off the tan I'd gotten while we kayaked. It seemed a little silly to get redressed if we were heading to bed, but I wasn't ready to stroll out in front of Luke fully naked.

When I left the bedroom, he was leaning against the wall, waiting for me. He took my hands into his. "You're nervous."

My stomach rolled a few times, but not in a bad way. "I'm not."

"You were twisting your fingers together. Over and over."

I looked down. Sure enough, I had been fidgeting, scraping my nails over the insides of my fingers, even as he cradled my hands in his. I straightened my fingers and raised one eyebrow. "See, not moving them at all." I nodded down at my perfectly still hands.

He smiled. "Because I'm holding them."

"So. I guess you can calm me down then."

"I have the perfect solution." He guided me to the couch.

"Is that right?" It had been a long time, but more importantly, I'd never slept with anyone I liked as much as I liked Luke. I'd never *wanted* anyone like this. It felt momentous, like it was a more important decision than just something I was doing for fun.

Luke slid the strap of my sundress off my shoulder. "I like this dress," he said.

"I thought you might."

He slid the other one down next, inch by inch. "You smell so..." He stopped to kiss the skin on my shoulder as he went. "Good."

My nerves sizzled. I tilted my head back and bared my throat to him. "What do I smell like?"

He licked across my pulse point. "Lavender." He bit down, just the gentlest pressure. No one had ever taken this kind of time before the main act. "And sugar."

I let my languid body sink back into the couch cushions. I wanted to participate, and take an active role, but my arms grew lax as he put all of his attention into caressing my skin.

"I think I'll go from the other direction now," Luke said, resting his hand on my knee, just as he had last night. He moved his hand up my thigh, to the edge of my panties. He lifted the edge of the cotton with one finger. My skin prickled. My body tensed in anticipation.

He slid his hand under the fabric, raking his fingers across my pelvis until he reached the apex between my legs.

I sucked in a breath. "Luke."

"More?" he asked.

"Yes. Don't stop."

His warm fingers teased over my clit. They raked up and down, rubbing over my sex, which was becoming wetter by the second. I moaned as one of his fingers dipped inside for a second, then moved up to rub circles over my clit.

How was he this good? How could his wife have left him? No. I didn't want to think about him with other women.

He pulled his hand away and then both his hands were at the sides of my panties, tugging them off. "Let's get this off of you," he said, pulling my dress over my head. "As pretty as this dress is, I want to see you naked."

He shifted me, lying me down on my back on the sofa. "You're still dressed," I said, shoving my hand up under his shirt. I ran my hand over his hard abs until he yanked his shirt off and tossed it on the floor.

I'd imagined what he'd look like, plenty of times. It was clear that he had a great body, but he didn't show it off. He could easily be on the cover of any fitness magazine. He was the type of guy who had every right to post shirtless photos on dating apps. But he didn't. He kept his amazing body under wraps, fulfilling his duty as a father and as the town's sheriff.

He took a harsh breath when I grazed over his pecs. I pushed myself up on my elbow and licked over his nipple. He shuddered and took my shoulders in his hands. "I'm not ready for this to end."

I relaxed back against the couch cushions. I'd have to try that again soon.

"Let me look at you," he said. His large hands cupped my breasts. Then he moved them to frame my hips. "You're so small." A small frown line formed across his forehead. "And delicate. I don't want to get too rough. I'm so much bigger than you are."

"I like your size," I said. I liked who Luke was as a person, and if his looks disappeared, I'd still want to date him. But I wasn't going to lie. His size was a turn on for me.

"Just slow me down if I get carried away," he said.

I wouldn't mind if he did get carried away a bit. In fact, I'd probably like it. But I didn't think he'd go for that answer right now. "I promise."

He pushed my knees apart and got his hand back between my legs. This time he speared me with two fingers, and his mouth latched onto one of my breasts. He licked and sucked at my nipple, while his fingers pressed farther inside, pushing upward, rubbing against the perfect spot. He moved his mouth to my other breast, and his thumb pressed against my clit.

"Oh!" My muscles seized up. My stomach clenched as my sex quivered in a sudden rush. My orgasm washed over me in pulsing waves, and then I went completely limp.

I managed to get my hand up to his neck. "That was amazing," I said.

He pressed a hard kiss against my mouth. "Bedroom?"

I nodded. That had been perfect. But I wanted more. I wanted every part of Luke that he would give me.

LUKE

The sight of Victoria, sprawled out on her couch, with her dark hair fanned out around her head entranced me. I couldn't look away.

She was stunning, but so breakable. I hadn't been with many human women. Victoria was athletic, and in great shape, but shifter females seemed sturdier, and like males, they healed faster than humans.

The shifter females I'd been with, including my ex, had also been physically aggressive in bed.

They'd been vocal about what they wanted, and pushy about getting it. And I probably could have hurt them, but it would have been tough. With Victoria, I could easily harm her by being careless. She wanted me in the leading role, taking charge of what went on in bed, but I couldn't just let go and go wild with her.

She wasn't a passive person, but she was not demanding in bed. I didn't want to go too fast with her.

She looked up at me, with half-lidded eyes as I scooped her into my arms.

I loved carrying her. She snuggled into my chest. "Mmm," she said. "You still have on your jeans."

If things went according to plan, I wouldn't have them on for much longer. I laid her on the bed, where she snuggled into her fluffy pillows. "You undid me," she said.

"That's the way it should be." I pulled a condom from my jeans and laid it on the bedside table before I shed my pants.

Victoria rolled to her side and stared at me. I let her look. I was happy with my body, although I couldn't take all the credit. My shifter genes made it easy for me to stay in shape. I did my part though, lifting weights, running, and practicing martial arts so I didn't end up outmatched on one of my rare missions.

She reached out to touch me. She ran her hand across my stomach, then dropped it down to grasp my cock. "You're so hard," she said.

"Because I'm with you," I said. Arousal was a permanent state around Victoria. She wrapped her fingers around my cock. Her light touch nearly sent me over the edge. "Ah." I grabbed my cock in my fist to keep from finishing all over her bedspread.

She rolled onto her back. "I'm ready," she said. "Don't keep me waiting."

"Yes ma'am," I said. I got the condom on quickly and crawled on top of her. She lifted her legs to wrap around my waist. I slowly pushed my cock into her wet heat.

"That's perfect," she breathed. Her eyes fluttered shut. "Just like that."

I pulled back, then pushed in, keeping the rhythm gentle but steady. Her pussy tightened around me. I rocked back on my knees, and gathered Victoria close to me, lifting her off the bed, still thrusting into her body.

"Oh. Luke." Her arms gripped my shoulders, while her

head hung back. Her beautiful thick hair brushed my arms as I held her.

I held her with one arm and got the other in between her legs. I stroked her folds, making light pinching motions over her clit until she thrashed against me.

"Luke!" She came again, arching back into the bed. I bend forward to capture one of her round breasts with my mouth. The second my tongue licked against her nipple, I came, shuddering into her still pulsing sex.

I pulled out of her gingerly, but the condom didn't fare well. Shit. I grabbed the edge and held on as well as I could as I got cleaned up and tossed it in the trash.

"Hey, condom mishap. I've tested for STDs, and I haven't been with anyone in a long time, but I wanted you to know."

She pulled the sheet up over her body. "It's fine. I'm clean too, and I'm on the pill." She fixed a pillow under her head. "You wore me out." She grabbed my hand. "Sleep."

I climbed into bed with her. Spending the night with Victoria sounded like the perfect end to a great day.

Over the next few weeks, Victoria and I had one date after another. As she predicted, her working from home helped with that.

I found that the getting-to-know-you stage was fun. That was another thing I'd never had with my ex. It was impossible when you came from the same small clan, or maybe we just hadn't tried hard enough.

I'd tried to keep my dates a secret from the kids, but in our small clan, that was futile—they were clamoring to meet her.

On a Friday afternoon, one month after we'd met, I picked Victoria up for an early dinner. "What would you think about meeting the kids?" I asked as we settled into a booth at the diner.

"I'd love to," she answered immediately.

I was a little shocked I was going to introduce them to her so quickly, but it felt right.

"What would they like to do?" she asked.

"They love going out on the lake. Are you up for that?"

"Yes. That seems like it might be a low-pressure way to meet them. We won't be sitting and staring at each other."

"They're five and six. They're easy to please at this point. Fair warning, they are rambunctious." Rambunctious was putting it mildly. All bear cubs were more energetic than human children. They were stronger, faster, and needed more time outside. Mine also happened to be loud. Very loud.

I loved that they were inquisitive, spirited, and high-energy—most of the time. But if you weren't used to spending a lot of time around kids—especially kids who were actually bear shifters, a full day on the lake was a daunting prospect.

Victoria wanted to meet my kids though, and I would do whatever I needed to make the day fun for all three of them.

VICTORIA

*O*ne month, and one day.

That's how long I'd been dating Luke.

He *had* to be too good to be true. There was no way a man like him could possibly exist. Former military, elected sheriff, volunteer firefighter, and single dad? He had to have some horrific flaw I hadn't yet uncovered.

My dating life was great, and life in Arkansas was great too.

I got up each day and worked from home. I missed Aria and the rest of my employees, but we kept in touch with video calls. I'd actually done more design work than management, which was a nice break. Only instead of going to an office made of chrome and glass, I worked in the living area of this home. The floor-to-ceiling windows overlooked a small brook with rushing water. The grass was green, and the trees were leafy.

He frequently surprised me by dropping off breakfast, lunch or even dinner, if he was working late. He texted me, he called me and chatted on the phone and he sent me photos of random landmarks throughout the day.

Last night, he'd suggested I meet his kids.

I hadn't spent much time with kids since I was one myself. A few of my friends had one or two children, but they had nannies that kept the kids when we went out at night. I'd heard horror stories of kids hating the women their fathers dated.

One of my friends had even been subjected to pranks that rose to the level of *The Parent Trap*—she found a live snake in her bed, left there by her boyfriend's twelve-year-old daughter.

Hopefully, Luke's kids were too young for that level of mischief.

The doorbell rang. On my doorstep were Luke and his two kids, Beth and Adam. I opened the door, and Beth immediately wrapped her arms around me. "Hi, Miss Victoria!"

Adam gave a big wave and darted past me, running through the den. "Got any toys?" he said as he smacked into my window. He pressed his hands and face against the glass. "Dad, look! Water in her yard!"

Until then, Beth had been glued to my side, but she peeled herself away to join Adam at the window. "A tiny river!"

Luke lunged forward and pulled Adam away from the window. "Hey. Remember what we talked about? Use your manners." He pointed to the smudges on my window, which also included bluish-green streaks. "Adam, did you sneak candy?"

He beamed up at his dad. "Just a few Skittles." He held his little hands up. They were both shiny with candy remnants.

Luke bent down in front of his son. "Apologize to Miss Victoria for messing up the glass."

"Sorry!"

Luke held onto Adam's wrist while the little boy tried to

pull away. "Point me to your Windex, and I can clean that up."

"Oh, it's fine. I'll do it later." They were a whirlwind, but their excitement made up for any messes.

In the few seconds we'd discussed Adam's smudges, Beth had abandoned the windows and made her way out the back door. She clattered down the steps and raced straight for the creek. "We could swim here Daddy!"

Still holding onto Adam, Luke stuck his head out the door. "Beth! Not today, get in the car."

"Okay. Let's go," Beth said, reversing directions. Her small legs never slowed down. "I'm ready for the lake!" She took off for the car, racing around the side of the house.

Luke's smile was sheepish. "I should have warned you about how shy my kids are."

I'd been afraid of sullen silences, and dirty looks. "I'm glad they want to meet me." It could have been far worse. I promised myself that if I ended up with kids or step kids one day, that I'd never be the type of mom who lost her cool over messes.

The water at the lake was a deep blue. The sun beat down on us, warming us as we sped across the water in Luke's boat. I turned my face up the clear sky as the wind whipped through my hair. I sat next to Adam on the boat, and as we swayed along with the water, I was reminded of the summers I spent water skiing as a kid.

After cruising for a while, Luke took us to a small island with some gravelly sand and some shady trees. While we drove the boat, his kids wore lifejackets, but as soon as we were at the beach area, they ditched them.

"They're really strong swimmers," I said. Even Adam, with his small arms and legs, made powerful strokes.

Luke bit his lip. "Yeah. We're all athletic, in my family." He kicked at the edge of the water. "Wanna go in?"

It wasn't exactly hot in mid-May, but the weather was warm enough for a swim. "Of course."

Luke stripped off his shirt. I swallowed. This was the first time I'd seen him without a shirt on when we weren't alone.

His kids are here, you can't get turned on.

Too much attraction—a nice problem to have.

As soon as we were in the water, the kids were right on top of us. "Miss Victoria, can you throw me?"

Before I could answer, Luke interjected. "Guys, let me do the throwing. Why don't we think of something else to do with Miss Victoria?"

"Can you do handstands?" Beth asked.

"I think I can." It had been a long time, but I was willing to look silly to make Luke's kids happy.

"Handstand contest!" Adam shouted.

"Everything's a contest with their cousins," Luke explained.

For the next thirty minutes, we played with the kids. We did handstands and backflips, we floated, raced, and eventually snorkeled before they demanded to be thrown again.

I had to take a break, but Luke kept going. Beth begged for one turn after another of being thrown, and I got to see what she meant. Both kids would curl themselves into a ball, and Luke would launch them into the air. They'd stay in a cannonball position, and try to make the biggest splash possible.

I loved watching him with his kids. He stayed calm even when they were wild, and he was patient. It made me think I'd like to have a baby with him as well.

I pictured a little boy with his deep blue eyes and his tan skin. For an infant, I could design a nursery, and I could decorate with navy blue, with yellow accents.

I laid down on the blanket and stared at the sky. That was

a pretty far-fetched fantasy. Luke and I had been dating for a month, and I'd already started imagining having his baby.

Time for a reality-check, Victoria.

A reality with Luke was here, in Arkansas. It was obvious that Luke wouldn't be moving anywhere, not with his strong connections to his family and the community, and I didn't want him to.

If we did get serious, would I be willing to leave New York permanently?

I wasn't sure yet.

Once Luke got out of the lake, the kids ate about three sandwiches each and then fell asleep on another blanket, while Luke and I lingered over our food. "You said they compete with their cousins. You have a lot of family?"

"Understatement." He sighed. "I love them, but they are over the top intense." He poured me another glass of lemonade. "Now that you've met the kids, my mom and sister will be ready to meet you as well."

"That sounds nice," I said, but from the look on Luke's face, he didn't agree. "No?"

"I live on a street with my parents, my sister and her husband, and my brother and his wife. That's just the immediate family. There are countless extended relatives. When you meet them, my dad and brother will be reserved at first. But my mom and sister will be excited, and they'll get right in your face and want you to start coming over to hang out."

"I can handle strong personalities." I had worked with all kinds of people in New York. I got along with most. I'd be polite, and friendly, and Luke's family and I would get along well.

"You haven't met them yet," Luke grumbled, but he was grinning. He clearly adored all of his family. "They feel entitled to barge in on my personal life, because they've had to help me since my ex left. They take a few more liberties with me and my kids than they would if I was still married."

"That sounds normal enough," I said.

"Enough talk about my relatives," Luke said. "I'm more interested in talking about us, and what we're going to do the next time we're alone."

I blushed. "Your kids are right over there!"

"They're asleep. And it's not like they're going to see anything. I just want to talk."

He rubbed his thumb over the clasp on my bikini top. "If we were alone right now, I'd unsnap this." His warm palm moved up to caress my shoulder. "Your top would fall off, and I'd be able to see your beautiful breasts. I like looking at them. I like touching them too. Most of all, I like my mouth on them."

I pressed my hand to my lips. "Luke."

He leaned back and looked me in the eyes. "Do you want me to stop?"

I shook my head. "No," I whispered. No one had ever made me feel things like this. In response to his words, my head went fuzzy. My nipples tightened. The space between my legs throbbed. If we weren't in public, and his kids weren't with us, I'd want him inside me.

Luke *wanted* me, and he wanted me to know it. There was no way I wanted it to stop.

His eyes, hot with desire, looked down at my chest. "You're getting a tan line. I want to run my tongue across it."

I bit down on my hand.

"After I'd licked all over your breasts, I'd move down. I'd peel those bottoms off. I'd run my hands over that sweet little bottom. I'd pull you in my lap, and I'd put my fingers in you."

I bit down harder, suppressing a moan. With my free hand, I grabbed his fingers and squeezed.

He held onto my hand. He leaned in closer to my ear. "I

love your responses." He kissed my ear. "I want to be inside you again."

I gasped. "I want that too."

"I'll make it happen. Soon."

I sat on the beach towel, panting. I grabbed a water bottle and pressed it against my cheek. While I was still trying to recover, the kids woke up.

"Our grandma wants to meet you," Beth said. "Wanna come over tomorrow?"

I pressed my hand into the cool sand, still trying to ground myself. "I'd love to. I'll talk to your Daddy about it, okay?"

"Grandma makes a lot of food. You'll like her."

"I'm sure I will." Beth jumped, spraying sand everywhere, and I caught her in my arms.

I spit the sand out of my mouth and gave her a tight hug. "I had so much fun with you today."

She grinned up at me. "It was a perfect day," she said.

For the first time in my life, I'd neglected work in favor of my personal life. I usually worked twelve hours a day, and today I'd done nothing.

Now I was paying for it, as I tried to catch up on my to-do list. Having the owner of the company slack off didn't set such a great example for the rest of the employees, though I trusted that Aria had kept the business running smoothly, and I knew Aria would assure me that it was a much-needed break.

She'd be right—I didn't regret one second of choosing Luke and his kids over my company. Every minute I'd spent getting to know Luke, Beth and Adam had been worth it.

As I settled on the couch with my computer, I couldn't

stop a smile from forming when I thought about what Luke and I had done on that couch.

My smile dropped into a frown as I studied my inbox. I pulled the laptop screen closer to my face, as if that would help the subject line make more sense.

Hello Victoria Brantley.

I have gained access to your client database. I know that one of our beloved United States senators owns the Triple X company, which produces custom sex toys, and I will release this information to the public, complete with proof, unless I receive $500,000 from you by the end of one week. Reply to this address. I will send further instructions about how you'll remit the payment.

Bile scorched my throat. Time stopped. I couldn't get a breath for almost a minute.

I promised my clients complete privacy—it was part of their contract. Now some criminal had my information, and the capability to expose secrets. I had well-known clients that ran businesses they didn't want attached to their names —like the senator he mentioned, and countless others.

Would a senator be expected to resign over sex toys? Maybe, maybe not. It probably depended on the district. But saying that he wouldn't appreciate the exposure was an understatement. He'd also have the power to make sure I never worked again. Especially if it got out that he'd been the model for one of the toys.

I rubbed my hand over my face. My company was being threatened, and I was in rural Arkansas, far away from my employees.

My systems admin was going to flip. Why hadn't I hired a security analyst?

I put the glass of wine on the bar, untouched. I had no appetite, not even for merlot. My perfect day with Luke faded into gloom.

～

"You ready for this?" Luke asked.

I checked my reflection one last time. To meet Luke's family, I'd chosen wine-colored capris and a black tank top with white flats. My outfit looked nice, but my face was pale, and dark circles hollowing out my eyes.

I hadn't slept at all after I'd read the hacker's email.

"I hope so." There was no way I wanted to ruin our day by dwelling on my hacker problems. Luke dealt with real problems. He'd had to do a wellness check for an elderly community member this morning, and he'd been the first person on the scene at a serious car accident yesterday.

He coped with life or death every day, and he didn't complain or let it get him down. Yes, my business was in danger, and I was potentially going to lose my reputation, but no one would die. I had to keep that in perspective.

As we stepped into his parents' house, the muscles in my shoulders locked up. I had to open my mouth to unclench the tension from my jaw.

I rolled my shoulders. *You meet rich people all the time. Famous people. Powerful people. You can do this.*

"This is my mom, Cynthia, and my sister Jane." Luke beamed at them as he introduced me to his mother and sister.

They did not beam back.

Their eyes were downright frosty, and their mouths were matching flat lines.

Luke's grin dimmed a little. Luke nudged his mother, and she recovered first. She was an attractive woman, tall, but not quite as tall as Luke. She met my gaze with an imposing glare. "Hi, Victoria. Luke tells us you're from New York. Is it dull here for you?"

I'd expected curiosity, maybe hesitance, but I hadn't

expected open hostility. I pasted a smile on my face anyway. "Not at all. I'm from Arkansas, so I'm glad to be back."

"Why did you leave in the first place?" his sister asked.

Luke glared at his sister. "Jane. Be nice."

She rolled her eyes at him.

"My parents moved to Canada for work, and I didn't have any other family," I said. "I'd never lived in a big city, so I wanted to give it a try."

"Pretty big change, if you ask me," his sister said.

What was that supposed to mean?

"Jane," Luke said, "why don't you come help me unload the car? We've got about a hundred boxes of pizza waiting."

I turned my focus toward his mom. Most moms and grandmothers loved talking about their families. "I love that you all live on this street together. It must be great to have everyone so close."

"Mmm."

Was that supposed to be an answer? I had no idea what to say after that.

She didn't make me wait long. "Why were you using a dating agency?" she asked.

Now she was going to interrogate me? Getting defensive with his mother wasn't going to work. I smiled again. "The same reason Luke was. I was looking for the right person."

"It wasn't Luke's idea. It was mine. Did he tell you?"

No, he hadn't told me. I couldn't imagine why that mattered to her, unless she tried to keep a tight rein on Luke's life. I hadn't seen any evidence of that so far though. "That's really sweet of you."

"He didn't want to date. He's been saying he's fine on his own, all these years."

Did she want him to date, or not? Or was there something about me that offended her? "I've really enjoyed getting to know him. I think I'll go find him now." I had to get away from her before I said something I couldn't take back.

I found Luke out in the backyard talking to his sister while his dad handed out pizza slices. "Everything okay?" he asked.

I hadn't met a boyfriend's parents since I was a young adult, but I'd never expected it to go badly. I worked hard to compose myself, and make sure nothing showed on my face. "Yes."

He frowned, but didn't say anything else. A little boy about Beth's size came running up and jumped from a lawn chair, right onto Luke's back. "Raptor attack!"

Luke made a loud screeching noise, and started staggering around, mock crashing into the fence while the little boy squealed.

His sister turned toward me. "So you work from home," she said with no lead-in.

I stared at the dogwood tree in Cynthia's yard. The dainty white blooms shaded a picnic table, where Beth and Adam were eating. I wished desperately to be with them. "I do now," I said.

"Luke's a busy guy."

"I can see that. I admire all he does for the town."

Jane's posture went even more rigid than it already was. "He is *not* going to move to New York," she hissed.

Was that what they were scared of? That I'd whisk Luke away from them? "I wouldn't want him to."

"But if you guys get serious, then you'll have to move back here. Or more likely, he'll follow you there. Don't think he'll leave his kids behind though."

Okay. This had gone too far. "I would never think that. I can see how much he adores Adam and Beth."

"You don't have kids, do you?" Jane asked.

"Excuse me, I think I'm going to find something to drink."

I didn't wait for a reply. My eyes stung. I wasn't a crier, but his mother and sister obviously hated me. Inside the house, I found a bottle of orange soda and drank the whole thing at once.

Luke slung his arm around me. "Hey. You disappeared." He took the bottle out of my hands. "Not your usual."

"Just needed a second." I leaned into his strong arms. "I drank it as a kid."

"Okay. What happened?"

"Just worried about a few things at work." That much was true. No man wanted to hear his brand new girlfriend rant and rave about his family. The family that he cherished, and the same family he praised for helping him out so much.

"Victoria. Come on." He smoothed his hands down my arms. "I believe that you may have some work stress, but that's not why you're in here. I appreciate that you're trying to be diplomatic, but I know my mother and sister. Tell me what they did."

"They don't like me."

He dropped his arm and stood in front of me. "What did they say?"

"Are you sure you want to discuss this? Maybe we got off on the wrong foot."

He swiped his thumb over the corner of my mouth. "Little bit of orange soda left," he said with a faint smile. "Look. This isn't a networking dinner where you have to put up with a bunch of crap. This is my family, and I'm not going to let them push you around."

"Let me handle it for now," I said.

He kissed me on the nose. "I'll let it go. For now." He sighed. "My ex-wife was flaky. We were friends when we were young, and we started dating, if you can call it that, when we were teenagers. My family loved her. They made her a part of our lives, and then she left. It devastated everyone."

"I can see why they're wary."

"It's no excuse."

"They think I'm going to lure you away to New York."

"What?"

"Don't say anything to them yet. If they think you're on my side, then they'll get defensive. They're looking out for you."

"We'll see."

While I appreciated that Luke would stand up for me, it would make a horrible first impression if he confronted his mother and sister right now. "Just give it time. I don't want them to think I'm an evil vixen who's here to steal you away."

He wrapped his arms around me. "I think I like the sound of that." He nuzzled my neck. "My very own sexy vixen."

I pushed him away. The last thing I wanted was for his sister to see us making out. "Not sexy. Evil."

"You're sexy, whether you're evil or not." He took my hand. "Let's get out of here."

"I thought you'd never ask." Next time I saw his family, I'd be prepared.

LUKE

*W*hat the hell was my family up to? Day one of meeting Victoria, and my mom and sister already terrorized her.

I was pissed, and I wanted them to know it. But Victoria asked me to lay off. So I would, for now. Besides, I couldn't be totally honest with Victoria, not yet.

My mom was the one who called the matchmaker. She knew I'd end up matched with a human. But now that it had happened, she probably regretted it.

Our clan didn't have any rules about mating with humans, not like other clans did. But there was an unspoken rule about being careful. Really careful. Every now and then humans reacted badly. In the last few years, freaked out humans tried to post information online. Before the internet was a thing, they'd tried to go to the news.

So far, the humans had been the ones ridiculed, but it left the shifters feeling exposed. In my clan, there were no humans. Not because of any strong prejudice, but because it was easier to mate with fellow shifters.

Despite knowing all that, my mother had barreled along

and gotten me a date with a human. Now that I was getting serious with a human, my mom likely had second thoughts. And my sister was always a little controlling. She'd never admit it, but because she'd been such a big part of my life lately, she thought she was entitled to insert herself into my life.

They were about to have a rude awakening if they thought they could run Victoria off.

I showed up at my mother's the next evening for her after-dinner gossip session.

"So, what do you think about Victoria?" I asked.

My mother sniffed. "She's very pretty."

My sister scoffed. "She's ritzy. What makes you think she's going to be happy living out here with a bunch of hill-billies that deer hunt and swill beer all day?"

"First of all, you're describing half of our family, and second of all, Victoria is from Arkansas. She knows it's different from the city."

"What happens the first time she wants to go to the theater, or a big museum, or eat at a fancy restaurant? We don't have that kind of stuff here, not like that. She'll hightail it back up to New York, and then where will you be?"

Ah. This made more sense. My family was demanding, and borderline rude sometimes, but they weren't cruel. They were looking ahead, imagining another woman leaving me and the kids behind.

I plopped down on my sister's barstool. "We aren't mated. Hell, she doesn't even know I'm a shifter. Just give her a chance."

My mom slammed her glass down on the table. "It's a mistake to get involved with a human."

"Mom, you are the one who set us up."

"I know. But I thought you'd just go out and have fun. I didn't think you'd fall for her."

"How do you know I've fallen for her?"

"You're my son. You loved Delaney, but even with her, you never looked this smitten." She picked her glass back up and pointed it at me. "You need to be careful. Every single one of us is a shifter. We've never brought a human into the mix. There are a lot of concerns. Who knows if she can carry a shifter baby?"

"Mom! We just started seeing each other." Who said anything about a baby?

"Besides, she's rich. She doesn't have to stay here. She can go anywhere in the world. What makes you think Pine River will be enough for her?"

I took a deep breath. Getting angry wouldn't do any good. "Delaney was a shifter, and she didn't have a penny to her name. And that didn't stop her from leaving me. Pine River wasn't enough for her, and neither was I."

Fuck. I didn't mean to say all that.

I stood up and shoved the stool back under the bar.

"Oh Luke," my mom said. She moved like she was going to come hug me. "I'm sorry."

I stepped back before she could get to me. I wasn't ready to get over it. "I'm not asking you to trust her. Just be nice to her, okay?"

My bear rumbled, but he wasn't too upset. Strong emotions were a part of our life in the Thomas family but I was still pissed.

"You said something to them, didn't you?" I asked as I made sure the ice maker was full.

"Yes." Luke looked over from where he was stacking plates to take outside. "But, before you get mad, I didn't bring it up."

I started pulling glasses out of the cabinet. "So what happened?"

"They were worried that because you're rich, that you won't be happy here, and that you'll either leave me, or that you'll entice me into moving to New York."

"It doesn't take a rocket scientist to see that you'd never move to New York."

"Don't say never. I'd obviously bring the kids with me."

"Don't tell them that. If they thought I'm here to take their grandkids and niece and nephew away from them, I'll be a monster." I laid the wine opener out on the countertop. "And besides, I'm not rich."

"You may not be in the top one percent, but for Pine River, you absolutely are rich"

"I am not."

"Look around." He waved his hands to indicate my house. "You're renting the nicest house in Pine River." He laid his hand on my countertop. "Most people here wouldn't know a granite or marble countertop if it hit them. There are rich families in Fayetteville and Bentonville, but out here, there aren't. People notice that your clothes are a little nicer, and your car is more expensive."

"I rented this car. It's not even mine."

"Victoria. It's a BMW."

Point taken.

I exhaled. This discussion was getting old. We'd tried hanging out with Luke's family again. The second time was just as much of a disaster as the first. His mother and sister were polite but standoffish. His sister-in-law was nosy and asked how much money I made.

I'd thought they saw me as invading their home turf. So I suggested a party at my place. They could see that I was renting a house, and that I was trying to be a part of the town.

And I needed a distraction.

I hadn't solved the issue with the hacker. I hadn't told my systems admin yet either. A few internet searches had revealed that I was dealing with a seasoned criminal.

So I'd invited Luke, his kids, his parents and his sister. We have to entertain the extended family after I'd won this crew over. Which was looking unlikely.

As Luke helpfully pointed out, I'd rented a BMW when I first got to town. I didn't drive much in the city, and the car had appealed to me at the rental place.

When Luke's brother-in-law arrived, he'd been friendly, but he'd never made it inside the house. He'd asked to see the BMW's engine. I gave him the keys and left him to it.

His mother ignored me, choosing to stay outside and play with the kids in the creek. His father said a brief hello, but then never spoke another word to me, even though I was in and out of the house, bringing food to the deck where Luke and his dad were grilling the food.

"Where's all your food," his sister asked. I looked over to see her standing in my kitchen with two of the cabinet doors open. "There's nothing to eat in here."

"It's just me," I said.

"You still need to eat."

Luke breezed in. He closed the cabinets and ushered his sister away. "I bring her food all the time."

"You do?"

"Yep. She's hard at work here, and I'm always out driving around."

Jane glowered at her brother.

"Plus, Victoria doesn't eat as much as we do," he said.

"Are you calling me fat?"

Luke shrugged. "You're the one obsessing over food."

His sister lunged forward. Luke caught her and they began to wrestle. I stood with my mouth open until I realized they were laughing. "Help! Help!" Luke shouted.

Luke's father opened the back door and they tumbled out, dragging each other across the deck and then rolling onto the grass. Once they were outside, their kids joined in. Beth and Adam, and Jane's three kids jumped into the fray.

It was bizarre.

His mom and dad cheered. Jane's husband was still fiddling with my car. I closed the door. Luke had told me they were an active family. As an only child, maybe I didn't understand how siblings behaved. At least it hadn't been a real fight.

Fifteen minutes later, they came back inside. Grass clung to their hair and bits of flowers stuck to their clothes. I didn't want them to judge me. So I wasn't going to judge them.

"I made some tea and lemonade," I called out.

Within minutes, both pitchers were empty. And then they tore into the hamburgers that Luke and his father grilled. They ate and ate and ate. At dinner parties, I'd always thought it was much better to have too much food than too little. So I overbought for hamburgers. I didn't eat red meat, but I bought enough food for everyone to have two hamburgers, with a few left over.

Just like the lemonade, within minutes, the food was gone. The rest of the afternoon passed without incident, unless you counted the frequent grappling matches, water splashing, and dirt throwing. There was even some tree climbing, by adults and kids alike.

"Dad, can we have a sleepover with Aunt Jane?"

"Sure." Luke wrapped his arm around my shoulder.

They were a happy family unit. Maybe they didn't need me at all.

I wished I could say things got better with Luke's family. But they only got worse. I tried to make myself part of the community. I went to the library. To the post office. To the grocery store. Everywhere I went, there was a member of Luke's family.

In Pine River, he had parents, grandparents, a brother, a sister, aunts, uncles, endless cousins, and nieces and nephews.

Everywhere I went, one of them was present. They seemed to make up the entire sheriff's department, and the volunteer fire department. The dentist I tried was his aunt. The hairstylist was his cousin. The librarian was his grandmother. I joined a women's action group that handled fundraising for children in need, and his sister was the chair.

I wasn't asked to leave. No one was openly hostile. But

their reaction toward me was clear—we don't want you with Luke.

And Luke was their golden child. People came to him when he was on duty and off duty. If a nephew struggled to put gas in his car, Luke handed him a twenty-dollar bill. If a grandparent needed some extra attention, Luke made sure it happened.

He'd been willing to stand up to his mother and sister, but they were all bold personalities. What would happen if they wanted him to choose between us?

Even if our relationship continued to thrive, I couldn't just live for a man. I had to have my own life too. I didn't need all the galas and society events, but I wanted friends and a life of my own. I was already isolated because my company and my coworkers were thousands of miles away.

If I were to blend in here, I'd have to accept their reluctance toward me, or find a way to win them over. Half my business was in marketing. Surely I could come up with a public relations campaign that would at least make them tolerate me.

Most of my friends in the city saw their families once or twice a year. Luke saw his family every single day. A tense relationship was not going to work for me or him.

I tried to stay optimistic, but his sister was a constant reminder of our strife. When I attended the charity meeting, the co-chair asked who could deliver food to the local schools.

I raised my hand. "I have a flexible job. I'm happy to do it." The co-chair, thankfully, was not a member of the extensive Thomas family.

I made arrangements with the co-chair to pick up the food, but during the conversation, Jane watched with narrowed eyes.

Once the co-chair was gone, Jane looked me up and

down. "You're inserting yourself into our lives. You're making him get attached to you. But if you hurt my brother, you'll regret it. New York won't be far enough for you to run."

I'd been reading articles on how to handle toxic family members, but I had no idea how to respond.

I felt out of place. Like I'd never be accepted. If they hated me now, how would they feel if I were a stepmother to Beth and Adam?

How would his sister react when I wanted to keep Beth and Adam with me while Luke worked, instead of sending them to her house?

I couldn't imagine the reaction would be good.

How would they feel if we had a new baby? Would they poison Beth and Adam to resent me too? Would they reject a baby because it was mine? Stepfamilies were challenging. And I was up for loving Luke's kids. I'd do whatever I needed to do to make our lives work. But I wasn't making any progress with his family.

I was getting ahead of myself, but at this point in my life, it didn't make sense to stick my head in the sand. I needed to be realistic. Marriage rarely made hard situations better. It only made them worse.

That night Luke had a late shift. He showed up at my house at 10 p.m. I'd long since given him a key to my house, and the password to my security system.

Luke wrapped his arms around me from behind.

"I'm sorry," I said. "I'm not feeling great."

"Can I get you anything? Medicine? Food? Blankets?"

"You're a great nurse," I said. "But I think I just need to sleep."

"Did my family do something?"

How was he so perceptive? Tonight, I needed time alone. I had to deal with this hacker, and decide if I was going to keep seeing Luke. I was already falling in love with him, but if I was miserable half the time, was it worth it?

Luke's kids had to be his priority. And if his family hated me, that would be hard on him. I'd watched plenty of other friends go down this road. It was never pretty.

I didn't want to end our relationship. Luke was the best man I'd ever met. But maybe we needed a little break, so we could evaluate what we were doing.

I was in a town that didn't want me, and the hacker emails were weighing on me.

LUKE

*A*s usual, Victoria looked like a movie star. She had on dark navy pants with a bright yellow top and a big white necklace. Her dark hair was curled in ringlets today.

Her typical smile was a little dimmer.

Victoria was upset last night. That much was clear. She'd said she didn't feel great, and while that might be true, something else was bothering her. I wouldn't say that shifters have a sixth sense, but sometimes I felt like we were a little more perceptive with emotions than humans.

Her eyes weren't red, and her voice wasn't hoarse, but a melancholy aura seemed to hang around her.

I hoped tonight she'd talk to me a little more about what was going on.

"Hey." I kissed her on the cheek. "I thought we could do whatever you wanted today." "I've dragged us to the lake, kayaking, hiking, and to hang out with my family. Do you want something else?"

She smiled but didn't answer. I tried again. "Bowling? Mini-golf? Real golf? Fishing? Bike riding? A movie?"

"You don't have to entertain me all the time," she murmured.

"I like entertaining you."

"Why don't we go for a walk?" "I have this gorgeous back-yard. I should use it."

"Works for me."

I took her hand in mine as we stepped outside.

The late May weather was warm, and the air was humid. We rolled up our pants and waded through the clear water.

"Luke," she said, and I knew from the way her voice cracked that I wasn't going to like what she had to say.

I froze. "Yes?"

"I'm going to go back to New York."

"You need to check in with your employees?"

"No. I mean. I do. But I need a break. I need to get my head on straight."

"You mean you need a break from me."

"No. That's not it at all."

"Then what is it?"

"This has all happened so quickly. I moved down here, I met you, and I liked you immediately. But I need to stop and figure out what I want to do now."

"So you need to break up to do that?" This was like my ex all over again, just wrapped in a nicer package. Did I fall for a woman that didn't want to commit long term?

"I thought I'd find myself again down here. But I found you, and that's the best thing that's happened to me in a long time. But you're a part of this town, and so is your family. They're everywhere."

"Have they said something to you?"

"Most of them haven't said anything at all. But that's not the point."

"It is the point. I'll talk to them."

"You can't fix this. I know you fix everything else, for

71

everyone. But you can't force your mother and sister to like me."

"No, but I can force them to be nice. Or we can quit seeing them."

She wiped her eyes. "I refuse to be the reason you end a relationship with your family. One that you really value. You were perfectly happy with them until I got here." "Weren't you?"

"Yes. But I won't allow them to mistreat you."

"It's sweet that you feel that way. And I have no doubt that they'd listen to you, but they'd still resent me. And along with you, they are the backbone of this town."

I wasn't going to beg a woman to stay here. I didn't beg my ex, and I wasn't going to beg Victoria.

Damn it all to hell. My throat burned. "I guess this is goodbye then."

"Luke. I don't want to break up."

"Reevaluating is a pretty word for breaking up. I've been down this road. I'm not doing it again. No wonder my mom didn't like you. She saw what you were up to."

A tear slid down her cheek.

"Luke. Please. Don't leave like this."

"Bye Victoria. I hope you're happy. Because I'm sure as hell not."

I kept my fists balled up so I didn't punch a hole in my truck. I settled for slamming the door, but it wasn't satisfying. I only made it a mile from Victoria's when I had to pull over.

I couldn't shift here. I drew my arm back and punched a tree as hard as I could.

My knuckles scraped over the bark. The skin busted and bled. A few of the small bones cracked.

It was better than doing nothing.

It wasn't a great example by a public servant, but shifters would understand. We had to learn to channel our rage. If I hadn't done something, I would explode.

I shook my hand out and went straight to my sister's house. I was not letting her off the hook for this.

"What did you do to Victoria?"

"I don't know what you're talking about."

"Jane. I know you. Wipe that look off your face and tell me what you did."

"I may have spoken to her a few times about how she'd moved down here and inserted herself into your life."

"What the fuck. You had no right."

"I had every right. You look out for every person in this town, except for yourself. Someone has to do it for you, and that someone is me!"

"Look. You've been great, but..."

"Shut it. Delaney was a crazy bitch. You couldn't see her for what she was. We all could. We all warned you. You didn't listen."

"Victoria is nothing like her."

"She doesn't have to be like Delaney to be awful. She's going to leave you. She's going to leave you, and she's going to leave Adam and Beth. And then where will you be?"

She was right. Victoria was leaving, but it wasn't because she was flaky or unreliable. She felt out of place here. I knew my sister—if she'd set her mind to shunning Victoria, and making sure others did too, then it would be effective.

I knew my sister meant well. Hell, some of her frustration was justified. I'd been the one to treat Jane like a second parent to my kids. But right now, I couldn't look at her.

Fuck. My bear growled. He needed out. He needed to run. Fury rolled over me. I had to get away from Jane before I added a hole to her wall.

Before I was even home, my mother showed up.

"Sorry mom, I'm about to shift."

"I'll go with you."

"I need to be alone."

"Jane called me."

"I don't want to hear it."

"She was worried. We both were."

"People break up. It happens."

"We aren't people. She's not a shifter. How will this even work? Are you going to tell her? You haven't known her long enough to let her know what we are."

"Yeah, no shit mom. Thanks to you and Jane, she feels unwelcome here, and I haven't had a chance to get to that point with her."

I loved my mom, but I had to get away. Now.

I'd head to the forest, then I needed to see Victoria.

I wasn't going to let her leave town thinking I was too stupid to figure out what my mother and my sister had been up to.

VICTORIA

$\mathcal{I}$ pressed a cold washcloth to my face. My life kept going downhill at lightning speed. The guy I liked —more than any I'd ever met—had stormed out.

And I was being blackmailed.

After he left, I checked my email with dread.

The message from the hacker had changed.

He'd upped the stakes, at least financially.

Hello again, Victoria Brantley.

As you have not replied, I am upping the required monetary payment to $750,000.

From your database, I have learned that one of the country's most popular actresses, who frequently rants about corrupted lifestyles, runs a dominatrix business. A business in which she also participates. Will she enjoy her viewers finding out?

If I hadn't run Luke off, I could ask his opinion. He was the sheriff after all. Or would that be considered going to the police?

I dug my fingers into an aching spot on my shoulder. My shoulders had been up by my ears all day.

I wasn't supposed to tell anyone, according to the hacker,

but I was going to have to hire a security expert. The expense wasn't the problem. Even if I hadn't been warned, there was a risk. The more people I included, the bigger the chances that the information would leak.

I gave up kneading my burning muscle and I buried my face in my hands. My life had gone from a fairy tale, to a nightmare in a few short weeks.

If I didn't pay, the hacker would release all my records to the public. I might not be nationally known, but in New York City, people would know who I was. No one would ever hire me again. What good is a web design firm that leaves its clients vulnerable to hackers?

Tonight I didn't feel equipped to date. I sure didn't feel fit to run a million-dollar company.

I flopped down on the couch. I'd have to make a decision soon. The hacker had given me a deadline of one week.

I raised my head. Someone was pounding on the door. I pulled up the doorbell camera up on my phone.

It was Luke.

For once, he wasn't going to see me all put together. I had on an old t-shirt from college, and a pair of ratty yoga pants. I smoothed my hair back from my face and stood up. I wasn't going to leave him out there.

I unlocked the door and cracked it. "Hi," I said.

"Victoria. Can I come in?"

I pulled the door all the way open.

He lifted his hand to touch my cheek, but let it drop before he touched me. "I want another chance," he said.

"What?" My mind hadn't caught up yet.

"I know the things I said. I lost my temper, and I hope you can forgive me."

"I don't know what to say. It's not about forgiving you, but nothing's changed."

"I had time to think about what you said. I know my family's overbearing. I know they're difficult."

"Luke, this isn't just a case of your mom not liking me, but we put up with each other for a week at Thanksgiving every year. Your family doesn't just live here, they *are* this town."

"I want to make this work."

"I appreciate that. But if we're going to move forward, I have to be able to make a life for myself here too."

"You're right. You're a successful, independent woman. I wouldn't expect anything less. I'm not asking you to put up with anyone's crap. I want another chance."

"Of course I'll give you another chance, but we're going to have to make some ground rules. And I was never breaking up with you."

"Sure felt like it."

"I am going back to New York though, I need to clear my head." I wanted to have a chance of figuring this out without interference from his family. "Why don't you come with me?"

"I can't leave the kids that long."

Of course, he couldn't leave the kids behind. But was I ready? There was only one way to find that out. "Bring them too. Summer break is starting, right?"

"Yeah. They get out tomorrow."

"Perfect. We can show them the city."

"Are you sure you want them in your apartment?"

"It will be fine. I have a housekeeper, and I'm close to Central Park. You can take them to museums or aquariums while I'm working."

"I think that's a great idea. When do we leave?" Luke definitely seemed like he was ready to stand behind his words.

"Can you leave your job behind?"

"I haven't taken more than a day off in a row in years. My

deputy will enjoy the chance to run the office. Plus I can check in with them while you're working."

"Let's leave tomorrow." I knew I was taking a risk asking him to come with his kids but he was worth it and besides, how else was I supposed to know if this was going to work?

∼

When Luke bought his plane tickets, he paid for him and his kids to fly coach. When he found out I upgraded us to first-class, Luke only smiled and kissed my cheek. I'd had some bad experiences with men reacting to my money, but I refused to pretend like I didn't have it. If I were a man, no one would flinch at me providing an upgrade.

He crouched beside the kids. "Tell Miss Victoria thank you for the nicer seats,"

"Thank you," they chimed. "These are awesome!"

"They haven't flown since they were tiny. I haven't taken them on vacation since they were small, and we went to the beach. This will be their first time in a big city. They've been to Little Rock, Fayetteville, and Memphis. That's it."

"You guys are going to love it in New York," I told them.

Our plane wasn't huge, so there were only two first-class seats in an aisle. "Would you mind sitting with one of the kids?" Luke asked. "I think putting them next to each other is asking for it."

"I want to sit with Miss Victoria!" Beth shouted.

"I would love to sit with you, Beth." The flight attendants thought I was her mother. They asked me if she could have a snack, and they looked at me for approval when she ordered a Coke as her beverage.

I found that I liked the feeling of people assuming she was mine. Last night when I thought Luke and I were done, I hadn't let myself consider how much I'd miss Adam and

Beth. This was jumping way too far ahead, but I wondered if Luke would let me adopt them in the future, if we ever got married. In most cases, I'd settle happily for the role of stepmother, or bonus mom, as I'd heard friends call it, but because their mother didn't maintain contact with them, maybe adoption was a possibility.

I was too realistic to think it would be all sunshine and roses. But I bet we could make it work. I vowed that I wouldn't let Luke's family discourage me from pursuing this relationship. When we got back, I'd prove to all of them that I wasn't so easy to run off.

I knew Luke wasn't uptight, so I let Beth get the Coke she wanted.

Once we were in the air, she pulled a stack of tattered paper from her backpack along with a battered set of markers. She handed me a blue marker. "We can draw."

"What should I draw," I asked her.

"All four of us. Together."

If my heart could have melted, it would have. As it was, my chest tightened, and I had to swallow a few times. How dare Luke's family try to destroy the possibility of what we might have?

I wasn't going to let them win.

When I'd gone to tell Victoria I wanted a second chance, I hadn't expected her to invite me to New York. I sure as hell hadn't expected her to invite the kids.

But here we were in the Big Apple. I'd been here, but the kids hadn't. So we did everything. We rode bikes in Central Park. We went to the Statue of Liberty. We went to Macy's, and Times Square. She had a rideshare through her company, but she took the kids on the subway too, and Adam was fascinated.

She was in her element here. She was confident and knowledgeable. It made me even more determined that my family not try and diminish her personality back in Pine River, assuming I could convince her to come back. Now we were about to see *Mary Poppins* on Broadway.

"Let me get the tickets," Victoria said.

"I have plenty of savings." I didn't make the kind of salary that allowed a lavish lifestyle, but my house wasn't expensive, and I saved most of my money.

Victoria looked up at the sky. She kept her voice low. "I

want to. If you're okay with it. I want to use it on people I care about."

"Hey. Of course, you can." I patted her back. "We'd love it. Thanks."

She nodded quickly. "You're welcome."

I wondered if some city jackass had been insecure about her money. Or worse, jealous.

I held her hand while we watched the Banks family dance across the stage. In the back of my mind, I wondered if our relationship made it, if we should move to New York. I'd be able to find a job easily, either in law enforcement, fire fighting, or private security—I had contacts in NYC from my days in the military.

The kids would be exposed to culture in a way they never would be in Pine River. They'd have opportunities and education and experiences. But they wouldn't have family. And I had an additional concern. Not only did my kids need access to outdoor spaces now, they'd need a nearby place to shift once they were teenagers. Adults could go a week without shifting before the side effects started, but some teens needed to shift every single day

Living in a city was a real struggle for teen shifters. It wasn't really workable. But it was a nice fantasy.

In spite of that, I imagined informing my sister that I was moving. Her wrath would be nuclear.

I was going to have to talk to her. Yes, I owed her for all she'd done for me. But it didn't mean she was going to have a say in my decisions. If I had anything to say about it, Victoria was a part of our lives now.

"Look at that view." I kissed the top of Victoria's head as we stared out her window at the city skyline. I preferred the

Ozark Mountains, but this was an inspiring sight. "So glad you invited us."

"I'm glad you came." She spun to face me. "Kids asleep?"

"They are." I handed her a glass of her favorite merlot. "I checked on them. They're out cold. It's just us now."

"Mmm." She drew back. "Give me just a second to check my email, and I'll join you in the bedroom."

I carried my glass into the bedroom. I'd already showered. I went over to turn on the electric fireplace in Victoria's bedroom, hoping for a little romantic ambiance. It wasn't the same as having real logs burning, but it would have to do. And as a firefighter, I could appreciate the city not allowing real fireplaces in a high rise apartment.

We hadn't been alone much since we'd arrived, but the kids had passed out early tonight.

I heard her gasp. I went back into the living area, where Victoria sat with her laptop. As always she looked like a movie star.

She sat on her cream couch, wearing a white silk robe, with her dark hair piled up on her head. Little curls spilled down onto her neck. I wanted nothing more than to push those curls aside and kiss all over her neck, but she was sitting with her hand over her mouth.

"What's wrong?"

She shook her head a few times. "It's a security problem. It's pretty complex."

Ah. A common perception from people who didn't know me. She thought I wouldn't understand.

I didn't blame her. We hadn't been together long. Plenty of my colleagues, both in law enforcement and firefighting, were intelligent and thoughtful, even if they didn't have any formal higher education. But I was actually educated. If I didn't have the high-level physical needs of a shifter, I'd probably be working at a desk for the CIA right now.

"Tell me anyway?"

I saw her hesitate and a look flitted across her face like one I'd seen for the past few days. I knew she was holding something back. I just hoped it didn't have anything to do with us.

"A hacker has been sending me messages. He's demanding money. Now he's upped the threat to a million dollars." She tugged at her hair, sending more of the tendrils down her neck. "I didn't deal with it when I should have. I should have hired a security analyst years ago. But I didn't. And now he's threatening to reveal all of my clients' personal information. Information I'm contractually bound to keep confidential."

"If he or she leaks this information, I'll lose everything. I'll be sued." She shook her head again. "Other businesses protect themselves against this. I didn't."

"I'm sorry."

"No, I'm sorry. I wanted this to be a nice vacation for us, but I'm going to have to bail on our plans tomorrow and deal with this."

"Come with me." She didn't ask, but got up and followed me into the shower stall. Luckily it was huge, so I could turn the water on, and we'd mostly stay dry.

"Why are we in here?"

"You know I was in the military?" When she nodded, I kept talking. "I'm not active duty now, but I'm still part of a special forces unit. I do missions a few times a year. So in situations like this, I'm always going to act in the most extreme, paranoid way possible."

"I don't understand."

"He or she could have easily hacked into your laptop's camera. They could be recording. And they could have access to your security cameras. I just want to tell you all of this in here, so no one else finds out."

"Even if he was never in my apartment or my office?"

"Absolutely."

Her face crumpled. "Fuck."

"Hey. I doubt he's made it that far." I leaned in closer to her, trying to block her from the spray misting us. "Want me to take a look?"

"At what part?"

"I went to West Point. I was trained as an intelligence officer before I joined the elite unit I served in. I'm not proficient in coding these days, although I know the basics. I can't pretend I understand the hacking, but I have contacts who do." I put my hand on her cheek and wiped away a droplet of water. "If you let me take a look, I'll know who to call."

"I don't know what to say. I feel really stupid right now that I didn't know any of that about you."

"I don't talk about it much," I said. "You don't have to apologize for thinking I was an uneducated hick."

"Luke!" She gave me a light slap on the arm. "I do not think that. And the hacker said I couldn't call the police. So I didn't want to involve you, and have him think I was reporting it." She shrugged. "So I did nothing. Which is not like me at all." She lifted her chin. "I want to handle this. Now."

"We aren't going to call the police, although depending on how sophisticated your hacker is, he could know I'm a sheriff."

He'd easily find the information about my work as a sheriff, but finding my military work would be much harder. "Some do thousands of these messages as spam, and they don't have any information. But your hacker's shown that he does."

"Yes. He has very detailed, very specific information."

"Have you received any weird attachments lately?"

She quirked her lips, tapping them with her fingers.

"No. I know better than to click on links or open

attachments."

"The email could very easily look like it was from someone you know. Imitating email addresses is how they get in. The email looks legitimate, and you click to open, the virus is released. Then the hacker has access to all your data, and you don't know anything has happened."

She stopped to think, staring into space. "Son of a bitch!" she shouted. "I knew this was weird. The day I moved to Arkansas, I got an email from my CFO. She hardly ever uses email, and she knew I was leaving—She joked that she was going to use my office! She doesn't like waiting on responses —she'd have texted me." She took a breath. "In the email, she said it was a document about a meeting we'd had. But it wasn't, it was an article that anyone could get."

Victoria tipped her head into the spray. "God, I'm an idiot."

I grabbed her hand. "You are not. Thousands of people fall for this."

"I've sat through lectures on this at conferences!"

"It doesn't matter. These people are good at what they do." I squeezed her hand. "The guys I know will be much more effective than the police." I winked at her. "Less red tape."

"Will it be legal?"

"They all have high government security clearances, so I'm pretty sure it will be."

I wiped my face off with one of her plush towels, and headed for the small bag I carried everywhere. First, I put tape over her laptop camera. Next, I set up a small jammer in the apartment. I was going to have to make a phone call, and I didn't want to do it in the shower.

"I'm going to disable your security system too. Before we leave, I'll set one up for you that can't be easily hacked."

I pulled out my burner phone, the one I carried in case I

got called in to help my former military unit.

Victoria gaped at it for a few seconds, though it was the least shocking thing I carried.

Jim picked up on the first ring. "Hey, man. It's Luke. I'm in the city. Do you have a minute?"

"What do you need?"

Jim never beat around the bush. I gave him a quick explanation of Victoria's situation. "Can you trace my location?" I asked. I really didn't want to give her address out, not with my kids here too.

"I'll be there in twenty," he said.

"One of my contacts is coming by. His name is Jim, and I trust him completely. I'd normally leave now and go meet him, but I don't want you and the kids to be here alone." I lowered my voice. "Listen." I didn't want her to see me holding a gun and flip out. "I have a handgun. I'm going to get it out, but I'm not going to load it unless there's a reason."

Her mouth dropped open. "How did you get that through the airport scanners?"

"I didn't. It's registered through the government. I'm allowed to carry it on planes."

"Wow. You have a whole other life I didn't know about."

Shit. *Fuck.* I had to tell her soon about the shifter thing. Because if she thought my government-sanctioned gun and my contacts in the military were scandalous…

"I don't mean to imply you should have told me. I mean. Look at me." She gestured toward her laptop. "I got the first email on the day I moved to Arkansas. I didn't tell you either."

She threw her arms around me. "I'm grateful you're here to help me with this. I don't know what I'd do if I didn't have someone I trusted right now."

I was going to have to make sure I was worthy of her trust.

VICTORIA

"**T**hank you so much," I said. It wasn't possible right now, but I wanted him. I was tempted to slide to my knees and pop the button of his jeans open. I'd done that before, used my mouth on a man, but I hadn't enjoyed it much. With Luke, I wanted it. I wanted to taste him, to feel him hard on my tongue. I had never talked dirty, but I'd read about it. I took a deep breath. "I want you in my mouth," I whispered into his ear, giving it slight nip.

"Later," he groaned. "Or I'm going to call Jim and tell him not to come."

"Right," I said. "We'll have to pick up where we left off."

"I like it when you say what you want."

I nodded. "It's something I've gotten better at over the years." I gave him one last kiss. "I'm going to get dressed." I couldn't meet his friend wearing a silk robe.

Luke nodded, and he went to stand by the door. He was fully dressed, down to his shoes. He held his gun in his hands, and his burner phone was in his pocket. I supposed he was always ready for whatever might happen.

Before long, I heard the doorman saying someone was here to visit. Luke buzzed him up.

His friend was the same height as Luke, but bulkier, and he didn't have the easy smile Luke wore. "Miss," he said to me. "Let's see the computer."

I handed it over and showed him the email that I thought had come from my CFO. He sat at my dining table and scrolled through my email. He pulled a flash drive out of his bag, and he took a photo of my screen. "You haven't told anyone but Luke?" he asked. "No one? Not an employee? Not a friend?"

"No one at all."

He stood up. "I'll take care of it. I set up a remote monitor on your laptop. I'll see any emails you send or receive. May take me a couple of weeks to find whoever this is and resolve it."

"I can't thank you enough. Is there any way I can repay you?"

He slapped the back of Luke's head. "Keep this one out of trouble."

"Luke? He's pretty much the definition of the perfect citizen."

"Hmm. He's got you fooled with that pretty face. See you," he said with a backward wave to me.

"You're just jealous because you can't find a date with that ugly mug," I heard Luke say as he walked Jim out.

"If you want to go spend some time with him, please do," I said when he came back up.

"Nah. I see him often enough on missions. Besides, I wouldn't give up a minute with you."

"Thank you for helping me. I'm used to being the problem solver and this threw me." I didn't think I'd ever stop being rattled over the invasion into mine and my client's privacy.

"I may not always be able to help, but I'll try."

"Now. About what I said earlier." I pushed my hand down to rub over the front of his pants. Within seconds, his erection was rock solid. "How does that sound?"

He let his head fall back. He grew harder under my touch. "I will never turn down an advance from you, Miss Brantley."

I tugged on his shirt. He yanked it off. I kissed his neck, his chest, and then licked over his nipple.

He groaned. I licked the other, laving it with my tongue. He groaned again, and swayed to the side, putting his hand up against the wall.

I kissed down his strong chest, and over his defined abs. I could stop and look at him for much longer, but I didn't want to wait to get him in my mouth.

I unbuttoned his jeans, then I unzipped them. He brushed his hand over my hair. Then he shoved his pants and underwear off and tossed them aside. He stood in front of me, naked, his hard cock jutting out toward me.

I bent to rest on my knees. I wrapped my hand around his cock and brought my mouth forward. I licked up and down, savoring the way he moaned and rocked forward. He moved until his back was against the wall. "Victoria. I won't last long."

I opened my mouth and closed it over his cock. I slid up and down, taking as much of it as I could. I recalled the many women's magazines I'd glanced through. I'd always scorned any articles that weren't business-related, but I remembered reading that humming felt good for a man.

I sucked in, then hummed. Luke jerked, and threw his head back into the wall.

The combination of his reaction, plus the feel of his heavy cock in my mouth sent electricity through my veins. My sex grew wet and ached for him. I'd never touched myself during sex with someone else, but I wanted to pull my panties down and push my fingers inside. I didn't—I wanted to wait for Luke's fingers, and Luke's cock.

He threaded his hands through my hair. "You're amazing. But I can't last." He tugged me up to stand in front of him. He put both hands on my face and kissed me. I knew he could taste himself in my mouth.

"I want to put my cock in you." He stuck his hand in my panties and dipped his finger into my core. "You feel ready."

"I'm wet. I'm ready for you." I pushed my body against his.

He grabbed me pulled my legs around his waist. "I need to be in you."

He laid me on the bed. He grabbed a condom from the bedside table and rolled it on. He pushed my legs apart. "I could look at you all day," he said. "But I won't make it that long." He bent forward and licked over my folds. "You are the best thing I've ever tasted."

I pushed him away. "Stop. I'm close too." I yanked on his shoulders. "Get up here."

He crawled onto the bed and laid down on his back, and he tugged me on top of him. He lifted my hips, positioning me over his waiting cock. I slid down, letting his hardness fill me up.

I rolled my hips, swiveling. I rose up, and slid down again, relishing the friction of his largeness against my sweet spot. My head went fuzzy, as the pleasure shot through every cell in my body. I had never felt like this before.

"Damn. You are gorgeous," he said. He grabbed my hips, and held me in the air, while he thrust up into me. He sat up, getting his mouth on my breast. He sucked and licked my nipple. "Touch yourself," he said. "I want to see."

I licked my lips. I could do this. I pushed my hand between my legs. My pussy fluttered with need. I rubbed over my slick folds, while Luke stared down at my hand moving where our bodies met. "I will be thinking about this tomorrow," he said.

That sent me over the edge. My sex pulsed and trembled, squeezing Luke's cock. He followed me over, thrusting up one last time. "Victoria," he breathed.

I laid my head on his shoulder, with his body still in mine. I was thirty years old, and I was falling in love for the first time.

LUKE

*W*atching the sunset in the Ozark Forest would never get old.

Victoria leaned into my side. "I loved being in the city again, but I'm glad to be back."

"Same here," I said.

After being away from their cousins for a week, my kids had been desperate to see their cousins, so my sister agreed to take the kids overnight. Victoria and I decided to go on a sunset hike in the forest. We wanted to try the Sixty Foot Falls Trail, which was a little farther away from Pine Valley than I usually traveled to hike, and it was marked moderate to advanced which appealed to us both.

The yellow-red streaks of the setting sun stretched across the sky, but I was distracted.

I had to tell Victoria I was a shifter. I just had to find the right time.

The trail was overgrown, so we walked separately. I went first, making sure stray branches hit me in the face instead of her. We grinned at each other once we made it to the falls. I turned my face toward the water, letting the cool air from the mist rush over me.

I didn't see the rock but I heard Victoria's shout.

A rockslide sent a boulder tumbling straight toward her.

I jumped, throwing myself in the air.

I didn't get to her in time.

She scrambled backward to get away, but slipped into the spring. Now she was trapped, with her legs half in the cold water.

I crouched next to her carefully, making sure I wouldn't dislodge the rock and crush her.

"Victoria. Is the rock's weight on you?"

"No." Her teeth were already chattering. "It cut my leg, but I'm farther down. The rock's just resting against the others." So far so good. She was really lucky.

"Did you hit your head?"

"No. Just my elbow." She held up her arm, which was scraped raw.

"I'm going to try and push this off. You stay still unless I say so."

I tried everything I could think of, but I couldn't get the boulder off. I got a branch, and tried to use the leverage to pry it off. No luck. I pushed with my back and with my arms. Nothing. It didn't budge. I wiped my forehead.

I check my phone. "No reception," I said. Victoria's phone was in her pocket, submerged in the clear spring water.

"You're going to have to go get help," she said.

"I'm not leaving you up here." Fuck no. "There are bobcats, snakes, and who knows what kind of people."

She wrapped her arms around herself, wincing as her hand touched her scraped elbow. "I don't see that we have a choice."

We did have a choice. As a bear, I'd probably have no trouble shifting the rock.

My bear wanted the rock off of her—now. He didn't care about anything but making sure she was safe.

Settle down. I have to explain this to her first, before you haul off and make a spectacle of yourself.

I bent down next to her again. "I have something to tell you. I was going to tell you soon, but it's hard to talk about." I didn't give her a chance to ask me if this could wait. "I'm a shifter. I can transform myself into a bear."

"What? Did you hit *your* head?"

"I don't want to shock you. You're already trapped under this rock, so I want you to know, before I turn into a giant bear and push this rock off of you."

"Luke, please be serious. I really need you to go down to the station and get help. I'll be fine until you get back."

"You don't believe me. That's fine. Just take a deep breath." I pulled my shirt off and dropped it on a rock.

"Why are you getting undressed?"

"So I'll have clothes when I carry you down this hill. Things will only get worse if hikers see a naked man carrying you away."

"Luke! Stop it!" Her voice held a note of hysteria this time.

I shed my pants. I couldn't blame her that she didn't believe me.

I looked one more time at her striking face. This might be the end of our relationship.

I shifted to my bear form.

Victoria screamed. Her eyes widened and her hands came up to her mouth. Her breathing, already too fast, sped up even more.

There was nothing I could do to reassure her, but I could get the rock off of her. I made one circle around the rock, trying to make sure I would roll it off of her, and not crush her with it. I thought I'd get the best leverage by using my shoulders, instead of pushing with my paws.

I pressed my right shoulder against the rock and leaned all my bear's weight against it. I felt it grind against the ground. I kept pressing. It took all of my strength to keep the rock where it was, and not let it fall back where it had been. I panted. I wouldn't let it trap her again.

Finally. I felt the rock shift enough that it rolled, enough for Victoria to get free.

I growled, and kept pushing. With one last shove, the rock flipped over and smacked the ground with a loud thump.

Victoria had not moved. She sat on the ground, staring up at me, not blinking. Not only was she breathing hard, her heartbeat pounded at a rapid pace.

Her leg was bloody, but it looked scraped or cut instead of broken. It looked like a few stitches should fix it. Thank God.

I backed away from her to shift. Back in human form, I got dressed.

I knelt by her. "Hey. You doing okay?"

"I don't know what to say."

She was still speaking to me; that was a good sign.

"I'm going to touch your leg, okay?"

Now that I was closer, I could see that no bones were visible. There was one deep gash, but it wasn't gushing. I ran my fingertips along the skin, but I didn't feel any swelling.

I cursed myself for not carrying a first aid kit into the woods. I did have a backpack with one small roll of gauze in my car. I'd never needed it with my kids, but it was more of a habit from being a first responder. Humans carried water, Benadryl, first aid supplies, and snacks.

I'd never been human, but I knew what they needed to survive. I should have planned. "I think we can wait to wrap this up until we get to my car," I said. "I'm going to pick you up."

She didn't flinch away when my hands brushed her skin.

Her scent was faint, but she still smelled of lavender and sugar. Would this be the last time I got to lift her and hold her close?

What if she couldn't live with me being a shifter?

VICTORIA

I didn't curse often. It was ingrained in me, by my very southern grandmother, that a lady didn't curse. I didn't agree, but the avoidance stuck with me.

I was back in Arkansas, and my grandmother was gone, but what the fuck?

Luke could turn into a bear.

I had lived in New York City for a long time. I'd traveled internationally. I'd had A-list clients who wanted a website made for the BDSM books they wrote. I really thought I'd seen it all, and that nothing could shock me.

I was wrong.

Really fucking wrong.

Now I was cursing again, if only in my head.

Luke took me to the clinic in Pine River. There was no hospital, but there was always a doctor on duty. Thanks to his status as the sheriff, the nurse worked me in immediately, and I didn't have to wait for a minute longer than necessary.

After ten stitches and a tetanus shot, I was ready to go.

I still hadn't spoken to Luke. He drove me home, and I let him help me inside. I hadn't processed almost being smashed by a rock, because I was stuck on the fact that my boyfriend was a bear.

I wasn't any closer to making sense of it.

I sank onto my couch.

"Can I get you anything?" Luke asked.

"You can tell me what just happened."

He sat down on my hearth. "I'm a shifter."

"I see… but what does that mean? Do you shift at will? Does it only happen when you need it? Were you born like that?"

"Yes, I shift at will; I can do it whenever I choose. Yes, I was born a shifter."

Something clicked. "Wait. Is everyone in your family shifters?"

"Yes."

"So that's why your family hates me."

He covered his face with his hands. "They don't hate you."

"Luke. They do."

He dropped his hands to his sides. "They've been obnoxious. But they really are touchy about my ex."

My leg began to ache. A persistent ache, and I still couldn't get warm. It might be June, but that water was icy. "Don't try to tell me they're okay with you dating a human."

"They'll get over it. I'll make sure they do."

My stomach dropped. I'd imagined having a baby with Luke, more than once, although I'd kept that to myself. If shifters inherited their ability to transform, did that mean my baby would be a shifter?

If we stayed together, would his family shun me forever? Would they reject my baby because his or her mother was human?

Could we even have a baby?

I was getting ahead of myself. Right now, there would be

no activity that would lead to a baby. "You can't make them get over it," I said.

He stood, and started pacing. "I can, and I will."

"Right. I'm sure they'll listen." I was clenching my jaw so hard I had to deliberately relax it. "I feel like a real idiot. I was bending over backward to try and build a relationship with your mom and sister, and the other thousand members of your family, but I wasn't dealing with a level playing field. I was never going to be accepted. They'd always resent that I'm human."

How many times had someone been standoffish because they didn't trust a human in their mix? "Were they afraid you'd tell me?"

He gave an exaggerated sigh. "It's complicated," he said.

"Complicated?" I huffed. "If you didn't think you could trust me with this, then why did you keep asking me out?"

"I do trust you."

"Doesn't look like it."

"You didn't exactly share your issues with me either."

"Do not compare this to my hacker problem!"

"Why not? You didn't tell me on purpose. You kept it to yourself, until you realized I was useful."

I shifted my weight. Now the pain in my leg had reached a full-on throb. "You are full of it! That is not what happened."

Luke's handsome face twisted into a scowl. "You thought I was a moron. And the minute things weren't perfect, you bailed and planned to run back to New York."

"I did not bail on you! Your family is a miserable bunch of assholes. And you being half bear is not even remotely the same as me having a work problem. Not even close. So don't kid yourself." I glared at him. "We slept together. Several times. If I got pregnant somehow, would the baby be a shifter?"

"Yes."

"Yes, definitely, or yes maybe?"

He stopped pacing long enough to face me. "Yes. One hundred percent. The shifter genes are always dominant."

He had a lot of nerve, keeping something that big from me. "A baby would tie us together permanently. You may want to try and act like I'm flaky like your ex, but I would not leave a baby behind for you and your family to raise. So you brought me into this part of your life, without letting me know that my baby wouldn't even be human." He might be the hottest guy I'd ever known, but I did not want to even look at him right now. "I don't even know what to say. You need to leave."

Luke stepped closer to me. "Victoria. Listen, this has been a rough day, you…"

"No." I held up a finger. "You listen. You need to go. Now."

"Fine." He pulled the key off his key ring and laid it on the table. He walked out. "I'm gone."

"Good!" I yelled after he shut the door.

I stared at the gauze wrapped around my injured leg. Fuck being a lady who didn't curse— fuck dating, fuck Arkansas, and fuck Luke. I was done with all three.

LUKE

My actions tonight hadn't looked like it, but I was in love with Victoria.

I had been since we went to New York, but I'd been reluctant to admit it. When I'd laid her key down, it had snapped into place. I wanted to see her every day. I wanted to talk to her. I wanted to share my life with her.

I'd kept it to myself, I'd acted like a jackass, and now she'd dumped me. Again. But with good reason.

My bear was agitated. Even a long run hadn't helped. He wanted to dig, to bite, and to claw. He felt Victoria's absence in a visceral way.

On a Monday evening in June, I stood in my living room. My kids were at summer camp tomorrow, and tonight they were spending the night at Jane's. Tomorrow, I had the entire day off. And I had nothing to do.

My burner phone rang.

"Luke Thomas here," I said.

"I found them," a deep voice said.

"Hi Jim," I said. "You said them? There's more than one hacker?"

"Yep. A man and a woman. Both young."

"Where are they?"

"Brazil. I've got an assignment this week, but I can go next week. Take care of this in person."

"I can go now," I said. I was desperate to do something besides sit at home alone and dwell on how I'd screwed up my life. "Send me the details."

"Fine. I'm going to assign this to you as a contractor. These people are a threat—they could attack the government next, so I'll handle the funding through the agency. You'll have to fly commercial, but I'll have someone meet you there with equipment."

"Thank you, Jim. I appreciate it."

Jim grunted. That was high praise from him. "You can pick up your plane ticket at the Fayetteville airport," he said.

"I owe you."

"You always do," he said.

If I could fix this for Victoria, I'd owe him quite a bit. Even if she never spoke to me again.

Cool air greeted me when I stepped off the plane in Rio. My Portuguese wasn't great, but I could say a few phrases, and I'd been to Rio on three missions in the past. As Jim promised, an agent was there to greet me, and he stocked me up on weapons and surveillance equipment.

The hacker's house was easy enough to find. It was gated, so I had to go in on foot. Getting in was almost too easy. Either they were arrogant and thought no one would find them, or I'd fallen into a trap.

As I got closer, I surveyed the property. I only spotted one surveillance camera. However, they had a lush garden, a glistening pool, and best of all, a view of Ipanema Beach and its sparkling water.

It looked like they'd been at this for a while. How many millions of dollars had they stolen? How many lives had they ruined?

I'd planned to go in through a window, but after seeing the lack of security, I tried the back door. Even their locks were nothing special. I used a tension pick set the agent had given me, and the door popped open with no problem.

I crept in, keeping my back to the wall. I gripped a gun in one hand, and a knife in the other.

I reached the living area without incident. The house was almost all white, with a sweeping staircase and modern features. A young man, who was maybe twenty-five years old, sprawled on a red sofa in the middle of the room. He appeared to be watching television.

I trained my gun on him. He startled when he saw me, but quickly relaxed back into the cushions. He gave me a lazy grin. "Did the government send someone in to stop me?" His accent was American. What a little asshole.

"I'm not from the government."

"That's what they all say." He winked at me. "Jessica, we have a visitor."

A striking young woman joined him. "What now? I thought you said no one would find us here."

"It's worked so far, hasn't it?"

She crossed her arms.

"You're going to delete every shred of evidence you have on Victoria Brantley, CEO and founder of Willow Oak Design, operating out of New York City. I'm going to stand here while you do it. Then you're going to wipe your server of every single target. I'm also going to watch that. You may think that I'm a dumb grunt. That's okay. You may think I won't know if you keep some of the data. You'll think you can cover it up. That's okay too. But you'll get another visitor eventually. One who will know if you've tried to trick me. And I won't like it."

The little shit stuck a cigarette in his mouth. "Sure man. I'll get right to it."

I grabbed the cigarette and crushed it. "Do you prefer a Brazilian prison, or an American one?"

He laughed. "Neither." He didn't get another cigarette, but he did unwrap a peppermint and start licking it. During all this, the young lady stood by, watching. "Listen, dude, waving a gun around might work on most, but if I start deleting data, it'll trigger an alarm. Then my colleagues will show up, and they are not as nice as I am."

"Then you better figure it out."

He rolled his eyes. "And if I don't?"

I was done reasoning with this asshole. "Go in the bedroom."

"Kinky."

"Shut up. Don't talk." I pointed at the woman. "You too. Go. Now."

She shrugged and followed him in there. I had to give it to them; they were brazen and utterly unconcerned for their safety.

These two had plenty of money that they felt immune. How many people had they bribed and blackmailed, here and in the United States? They had no doubt destroyed a lot of lives, and cost people their careers and their life savings.

Yet I wasn't going to kill them if they weren't violent.

Shifting had cost me my relationship with Victoria. I would use it to scare these two assholes, and maybe they'd think twice before terrorizing anyone else.

"Sit." I pointed at the edge of the bed.

Surprisingly they complied.

I stripped my clothes off. I was taking a risk by putting my gun down, but I wouldn't need it once I was a bear.

"Whoa, man. I didn't know we were having a threesome. "

"Shut up," I said, then I shifted.

The man's face turned bright white. The woman gasped and scrambled backward on the bed. The guy trembled, and I was pretty sure he wet his pants.

Not such a big talker now, asshole.

My five hundred pound bear knew these were the shit-heads that tormented Victoria. He roared in the man's face first, then the woman's. I shoved at the bed, with my shoulder, just as I'd pushed at the rock. The bed creaked and moved easily.

They both screamed and cried openly now.

"Okay. We'll do anything. Shit. Don't eat us," the man begged. Now he was sobbing. I slashed my claws across their curtains, ripping them from the wall. I pushed their dresser over, letting it crash into the wall.

I roared again as they dropped to the floor and cowered by the bed.

I tapped each of them with my paw. Then I shifted back. I got dressed and picked up my gun. "Now that I've smelled you," I said. "I can track you anywhere in the world. If I find out that you've ever hacked again, in any form, I'll find you." I leaned in. "And I'll eat you."

They nodded. "We understand," the woman said as her voice shook so much I could barely hear her.

"Good. I'll see you later."

I went back to their living area and planted a few bugs that Jim had sent for me.

I was ready to get the hell out of here.

I might not have Victoria, but at least I could get back home to my kids.

VICTORIA

I was in love with Luke. I knew it was happening, over the last few weeks, but I hadn't wanted to examine it too closely. No one person had ever evoked much emotion from me. No one except Luke.

I swatted a gnat away as I stood on Jane's front door. Luke's sister opened the door right after I knocked.

"Hi Jane," I said.

"Luke's not here," she said.

I'd already tried his office and his house. "Do you know where he is?"

"He's on vacation."

Vacation? He'd just taken off a week to visit New York with me. He'd mentioned several times that it had been years since he'd taken a vacation. "Where did he go?"

"He didn't say. Just that he's on vacation. If you'll excuse me, I need to make dinner."

Before she could close the door in my face, Beth came flying through the foyer. She rammed into my side with her arms out. "Miss Victoria!"

I held on tight. I had missed her.

Now that I knew she was a shifter, I could feel the extra strength in her little body. I wondered if she could already shift, or if that came later. There was so much I didn't know.

And Luke had told me nothing.

Not until he was forced to.

I was still stunned, but as the day wore on yesterday, the throb in my leg increased, but my anger slowly faded. Luke should have told me about being a shifter. But I could see now that it would be an impossible topic to explain. And at what point? Before we slept together? Ideally, yes, but that was our third date.

If I'd known his family had another legitimate reason to be concerned, besides his ex, then I'd have been more patient. It hadn't been fair to me, or to them, to force the relationship when I was missing a huge chunk of vital information.

But when it mattered, when I was stuck under a giant rock, Luke hadn't hesitated. He'd acted. Which is what I wanted in a partner.

How could I punish him for not telling me something so massive?

Would I have told him? He was right that I hadn't shared my hacking problems with him; not until it had gotten so bad I couldn't hide any longer.

"Daddy's not here," she said. "He went to Bayzil."

"Brazil," Jane corrected.

Brazil? My brain clicked on. He'd left his kids here. He wasn't on vacation. He was on a mission. What if he'd left to deal with my hacker?

Jane tugged on Beth's ponytail. "Hey, sweetie, would you mind taking the dogs out?"

"Sure, Aunt Jane." Beth was gone in a flash.

Jane pulled a package of steak from the freezer. "Why are you here?"

Because Luke would absolutely go after the hackers to protect me, even if I wasn't speaking to him.

I leaned on her countertop. My leg throbbed. "I know Luke's a shifter."

Jane dropped the knife she was holding. "He told you."

"More or less."

"So what do you want?"

I never ate red meat, but the sight of the steaks was making my stomach roll. I gulped and looked away. No way in hell I'd tell Jane that. "Nothing."

She snorted. "I'm guessing you didn't take it well from the grimace on your face."

"I had a strong reaction," I admitted. "But Luke and I can work that out. I'm here to let you know that I won't disappear on him. Even if things get hard." She looked at me but didn't reply. "I prefer us to get along," I said. "I don't know what to do to make that happen. What do you suggest?"

She picked her knife back up and started chopping onions. "Don't screw him over."

"I can promise that I'll do my best." I hadn't told Luke I loved him. I sure didn't want his prickly sister to be the first to know, but I had no choice. "I love him, " I said.

She glowered at me. "You say that now. Do you think you can handle us? We eat red meat, every single day. We meet every week to shift. Together. You'll never be able to do that."

I didn't want to pretend the differences didn't scare me. "I'll adjust."

She slammed her knife down and dumped the onions into a pan. "You know, the kids are already crazy about you. All they can talk about is the things you did with them in New York."

Maybe I detected a little jealousy. I could work with that, and try to diffuse it. "They had fun. But you were the first person they wanted when we got back," I confessed. "Maybe you and I could hang out sometime. We could get to know each other." At this point, it sounded like torture, but I was willing to try, assuming Luke wanted me back.

"I can do that." She placed the steaks on a tray before washing her hands. "I'm not that bad, usually. But you have to understand how this looks to us."

My stomach was rebelling again. "I get that. I'm asking you to give me a chance." I was not going to tell her we'd fought, or that he was on a mission for me.

What if something happened to him? It would be my fault. All because I hadn't been proactive enough to hire a security analyst. Lesson learned.

If I knew where in Brazil he was, I'd go after him. He'd come to me to apologize before we went to New York. I could do the same for him now. But Brazil was a massive country. If I knew how to contact Jim, I'd do that too. But Luke had called him from the burner phone.

I would have to settle for waiting.

"Do you want to stay here for dinner?" Jane asked.

Wow. I hadn't expected her to make an effort this soon. She wasn't smiling at me, but the glower was gone. However, I didn't want to push my luck, plus my digestive system was not going to be up for anything intense. "Thank you for the invitation, but I need to catch up on some work." I'd missed an entire day, thanks to our hike, my slashed up leg, and my fight with Luke. Although the fight with Luke hurt far more than any injury.

I also didn't want to whine to her, but I was also exhausted, and my stomach was rumbling unpleasantly.

Jane was polite as I left.

I drove home. I was drained, I wanted to see Luke, and sleep, in that order. As much as I appreciated him wanting to protect me, I hoped his mission was related to his service. I hoped it was worthwhile. If something happened to Luke because of the hacker, I'd never forgive myself. Nothing in my career was worth his life.

I wished I could tell him.

I sat down to answer my emails from Aria. My stomach went from rumbling to a full-on churn. I tried eating some yogurt, then some toast. Neither settled my stomach. I checked my phone. No messages.

I could send a text to Luke. Maybe he'd see it. If he was on a mission, he'd likely have his phone turned off.

How in the world did I start? I perched on the edge of my sofa. I couldn't get comfortable.

I typed and erased several versions. I settled on a simple message.

Please be safe. I wish I'd told you—I love you.

I hit send before I could second guess myself.

My nerves caught up with me. The acid in my stomach boiled over, and I ran to the bathroom. I vomited up everything I'd eaten.

My stomach still didn't settle.

I sat on the couch and stared at my phone. Working was impossible. If something did go wrong for Luke, I wouldn't even know. I hoped Jane would at least call me, but I wasn't certain.

I wrapped a blanket around my shoulders. I turned my phone volume up as far as it would go.

The nausea didn't end. I staggered to the kitchen and checked the date on the yogurt. It didn't expire for a month. I found a large bowl to serve as a makeshift toilet. It had been a decade since I'd thrown up more than once. I leaned my head against a cushion.

Please come home soon Luke.

LUKE

*A*s soon as I was done with the two little asshat hackers, I hung around for a few hours, just sitting in their living room. I got a kick out of watching them jump every time I moved.

Once I was sure they were sufficiently cowed, I got the hell out of Rio. Jim left me the option of an open-ended ticket, so I was back on a plane to Fayetteville within two hours. It sucked, but the travel time on a commercial flight was a lovely twenty hours.

While we were still on the tarmac, I put my burner phone away and turned on my regular cell. As soon as it powered on, a flurry of texts popped up, one after another. Most were what I expected—from my kids, and my family.

I smiled as I looked at Beth and Adam's crayon drawings of all of us watching a movie while in bear form.

I exhaled. There was a text from Victoria.

She told me she loved me over text?

That sounded ominous.

Had someone told her I was on a mission?

I hit the call button. As soon as I got the phone to my ear, a flight attendant appeared. "Sir, you need to turn your phone off please. We're taking off."

Damn it.

I quickly typed a message.

Are you okay? On my way back.

I was about to type that I loved her too, but the flight attendant was back. She squinted at me and pointed at my phone. "Sir."

Shit. I was on a plane with civilians. The last thing I needed to do was cause a scene in a foreign country. Sure Jim had signed me into his records as a contractor, but it would be much better if I didn't stir up any shit.

As soon as I left the airport, I called my kids and told them I'd be home in a few hours. I drove straight to Victoria's house.

"Victoria?" I called out as I knocked on the door. My bear wanted to break the door down.

I paced back and forth on the front porch.

He scratched at me, wanting out. He wasn't going to wait on me much longer before he went to look for her.

No answer.

Why had I given her back my key? It felt satisfying in the moment, but now I didn't have it. If she didn't answer, I'd have to call one of my deputies to do a well-check. If she had meant to break up with me, then she wouldn't want me in her house for any reason—she'd think I was abusing my power as sheriff.

I knocked harder. No answer.

I rang the doorbell.

My bear pushed again— it felt like he was digging at the inside of my head.

Okay, okay. I'll go around back. If we don't see her, I'll call the deputy to come check on her.

I stepped off the porch to go around the back of the house when the door cracked open.

"Luke?"

Oh, thank God.

Victoria's voice was softer than I'd ever heard it, but at least she was talking.

"Victoria." I ran to the door. I stopped short. She was as beautiful as ever, but her skin was white, with a grayish tint. There was no color in her cheeks at all. Even her lips, usually rosy pink, were colorless.

My heart stuttered. What had happened? Had those jackass hackers threatened her again? This time they'd get a lot more than me as a bear.

I wanted to hold her. "What's wrong?"

She swallowed a few times. "You better come inside."

"Do you need a doctor? How's your leg?"

She gave me the faintest smile. "My leg is fine."

She settled on the couch cushion and pulled a blanket tight around her.

I was going crazy. "Are you ill?"

"No."

She was killing me. I walked back and forth over her rug.

"Could you sit down?"

I sat.

"I'm pregnant," she said.

That, I was not expecting. A baby. Relief. Joy. Excitement. *Mine*, my bear shouted. He wanted to grab her and hold on tight.

Just give me a minute.

"Was this from the broken condom?"

"I assume it was," she said. "That was over a month ago. So the timing is right."

She had been taking the pill, but we all knew that didn't always work. I wasn't even sure if my being a shifter might have anything to do with it. I'd have to bring that up later. "How…" I had to phrase this carefully. "How do you feel about it?"

"I'm shocked." She frowned. "How do you feel about it?"

"Honest answer?" I asked.

"Yes. Please."

"I am over the moon. I would love to raise a baby with you. I would love to give Beth and Adam a little sibling."

She sagged a little. "I thought you'd be happy. But you looked a little weird."

"I was trying not to go crazy and grab you and spin you around."

She held her hand up. "Please. No spinning."

I took her hand in mine. "I'm sorry I was such a jerk before."

"I'm sorry too. I overreacted. I don't want to blame my hormones, but." She gestured down to her stomach. "I do feel a little more emotional than usual."

I motioned to her stomach. "Can I?" She nodded. I put my hands over her flat stomach. I met her gaze. "I love you," I said. I bowed my head until my face was next to her stomach. "I love you too, little cub."

Victoria sniffled. "You're killing me. I love you too."

"Can I take you to bed? Just to sleep?" I wanted to get my arms around her.

"That sounds great."

"If you're nauseated, there are some ginger lollipops at the pharmacy that worked great for Jane."

"Shifters get morning sickness?"

"Some. I'll ask her to drop some off."

"Then she'll know."

Oh. Maybe she didn't want my sister to be that involved

in our lives. If so, I was willing to compromise, but it would take some adjustment. "Do you want to keep it a secret?"

"No. Tell her. And tell her she's the only one that knows. Maybe it will help mend things."

That was very generous of her. I needed to talk to my sister anyway, and let her know how important she was to me, but also let her know that Victoria was my family now too.

"You know who else is going to be delighted?" I smiled. "Beth. Adam too, but Beth really wants a baby. I just never thought it would happen." I kissed Victoria on the nose. "I am so excited. I can't wait to raise this baby with you."

Two days later, I took the kids to the park "Beth, Adam. I have something important to ask you." I'd discovered it was better to have discussions when they were active. "I want to ask Miss Victoria to marry me. How do you feel about that?"

Beth was hanging upside down on the monkey bars. She gave a deafening screech and dropped to the ground. "Yes! I want her! Will she live with us? I want her to!"

Adam was halfway up the slide—climbing the wrong way of course. "That sounds fun," he said. "We can stay in her nice house again."

"I'm sure we'll go back to New York at some point."

The kids cheered. "She bought us candy there."

I laughed. "Yes. I remember." All of New York's culture, and my kids remembered the sugar.

"Can we go with you?" Beth asked.

"Where?"

"When you proposal!"

I laughed. "When I propose? How do you know that word?"

"Jennifer at school. Her sister got a proposal. From her boyfriend. They videotaped it and she let us watch it at our sleepover."

Okay then. At least my kids were on board. "Yes, you can go with me."

The kids were beside themselves. Glee poured out of every pore.

They delighted in helping me plan the proposal. I'd decided we were going back to the river where we first kayaked, and they both wanted to get down on one knee with me. I had to temper their plans—they wanted balloons, posters, and confetti. I think they'd bring a marching band if I'd let them.

Eventually, I convinced them that just the three of us, and the ring would be enough. They'd insisted on helping me pick it out. One of my aunts made jewelry, and the kids picked out a diamond in the middle, with their birthstones on each side—one garnet and one amethyst.

I hoped we hadn't gone overboard.

Jeez, now that I'd involved my kids, what if Victoria said no?

It probably wasn't the smartest idea to have let them come with me.

At least she'd know we were all in. There was nothing half-hearted about it. Yes, it was fast, but I was in love with her, I trusted her, and we were having a baby together. The long history I'd had with my ex hadn't done a damn bit of good.

I told Victoria the kids wanted to have a picnic with her, no kayaking this time. Victoria was still a little queasy, but she rallied.

She tried to help us set up for the picnic, but the kids wouldn't let her. They shoved her into a camping chair, and they very seriously went about the task of setting out plates with cheese and crackers.

"Daddy. I'm ready now. Do we have to eat first?"

"No. Let's do it now." I didn't want to wait either.

"Adam!" Beth tried to whisper, but it was more of a shout. "Get over here."

"Miss Victoria. We're ready." Beth gave a little curtsey. "Here's your plate."

Victoria sat cross-legged on the blanket. "This looks lovely." The three of us stood in a row, looming over her, watching as she took a bite of cheese.

"Are you all going to sit down?" She asked.

I coughed. I stuck my hand in my pocket. Whew. It was still there. I pulled the ring out. "Okay guys, now." That was our cue. The three of us got down on one knee.

Or we tried to.

Adam lost his balance and toppled into me. I caught him, but hit Beth with my elbow, which knocked her into the pitcher of tea, which dumped over into the grass.

I grabbed it and turned it upright. "Just leave it. It's fine."

We got ourselves straightened out.

"So. Now that you know what life with us is like. We have a question." I waited until I heard their little voices start shouting. "Miss Victoria, will you marry us?"

Victoria had both her hands pressed together, right in front of her face. She blinked rapidly, over and over.

"Is that a yes?" Beth asked.

"Of course it is!" Victoria held her arms out to my daughter. "Come here."

"Wait!" I snagged the back of Beth's shirt and caught her mid-leap. "Do not jump on her. You remember we talked about the baby cub."

Beth nodded. She took her role as future big sister very

seriously, but she was accustomed to flinging herself at her family.

And that's what Victoria was now, with or without the proposal. She was family.

Victoria waved her arm at Adam. "Come here, you." He joined in, and the three of them rocked back and forth in a group hug. Finally, they'd had enough hugging, and they both ran off to climb a tree.

I was still holding the ring box. I sat down next to her. "I hope that wasn't too much."

She patted her eyes with a paper towel from the picnic. "I can't believe it."

"I want us to be married as soon as possible. I can make it happen, however you want it. But don't feel pressured. We can stall with the kids if you need more time."

"No. I'm ready now."

"In that case." I got back on one knee. "Victoria Brantley, will you marry me?"

"Yes." Her voice was a hoarse whisper by now.

"I'm a lucky guy." I slid the ring on her finger. "They got too excited to tell you. But those are their birthstones."

"I want to adopt them. If that's something you'd consider."

"I would love nothing more. You're already their family. We'll make you their mom officially."

She sniffled. "Don't make me cry more. This was perfect. I can't believe you did all this."

"I want us to be a family."

"I want that too."

I wasn't going to make the mistake of letting Victoria think she wasn't wanted. It might be an uphill battle with my family, but she would never doubt that she had my full devotion.

EPILOGUE

"*B*aby Bennett!" Beth called out as soon as she was awake. "I'm ready to snuggle you!" Beth made her usual tornado through the house, but I managed to grab her before she made it out of the kitchen.

"He's still eating. He'll be done in a second." I handed her a plate with sausage and eggs. "You eat your own breakfast first."

In the den, Victoria was nursing Bennett. I plopped next to her on the couch and gave her a quick kiss on the cheek. "

"Remind me what we have going on today," Victoria said. Her eyes weren't even open. She switched the baby to the other breast.

"First is a soccer game for Adam." Who was a fabulous soccer player, and we all loved watching him play. But his games were at eight a.m. on Saturday. "Next is a school carnival for both kids at noon. It's a fundraiser." I thought for a minute. I'd blanked out on what came after that. I pulled my phone out and looked at the calendar. Ah. "After the fundraiser, Beth has piano, then we're supposed to meet my family for my cousin's birthday."

Victoria let her head fall against the couch. She turned to look at me. "Sounds like a good day," she said.

I looked down at Bennett, who'd fallen back asleep. I scooped him up, cuddling him for a few minutes before I swaddled him and returned him to his bassinet we kept in the den.

Victoria slumped over sideways. There was no way she could make it to the soccer game. I picked her up too, and took her to the bedroom.

"What are you doing?" she mumbled.

"Go back to sleep. I'll handle the soccer game."

"Won't be fair to miss it," she said, but she made no move to get up.

"I tell you what. You skip the soccer game, and come to the fundraiser. You escort Adam at the school, and I'll handle the baby. Problem solved." I pulled the covers over her. She was already passed out.

In the den, both Adam and Beth were making faces at the baby, whose eyes were open. At four weeks old, he couldn't play, but if he was awake, his eyes were glued to the two of them.

I could watch them together all day.

When we returned from the soccer game two hours later, Victoria was up. "We're ready," she said, holding up the packed diaper bag.

"Mom!" Adam tugged on her leg. "We won."

She stooped to hug him. "That is amazing. I can't wait to see the video that dad took."

Beth rushed to kiss the baby, and I pulled Victoria close. "You look gorgeous as usual."

"Thanks for letting me sleep," she said. "I even managed

to answer a few emails." She waved me off. "I know, I'm supposed to be resting. But it's still my company."

I kissed her on the head. "I wouldn't change you a bit. And you're welcome. You're going to need your rest to cope with this fundraiser," I whispered. "They have a petting zoo."

She blinked at me. "Yeah," I said. "It's crazy."

We looked at each other and smiled. My bear rumbled happily. He was as content as I was. I had three healthy kids and a gorgeous wife.

A year ago, I never could have imagined how much our lives would change for the better. I really needed to send a gift to the dating services we'd both used. Those matchmakers had given us both a happily ever after.

READY FOR MORE SEXY BEAR SHIFTERS? - READ AN EXCERPT FROM THE NEXT BOOK NOW

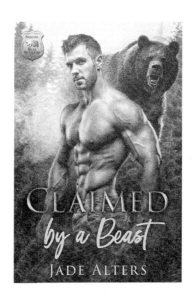

ADELAIDE

rigid air hits my face as I shoved my way outside. Ugh. My damp shirt clung to my icy skin. Still wet. Still sticky too, thanks to the angry passenger that tossed an open Coke can at me because I wouldn't let her take it through security.

As if I made the rules.

At the time, it seemed like too much trouble to change clothes, so now I sported half-frozen Coke on my uniform.

While the security officer escorted the crazy passenger away, I'd bitten down on my tongue and ignored her tirade of insults. I'd managed not to let a single retort slip out of my mouth, but it had been a close call. The unruly behavior would only increase. Thanksgiving was four days away and the holidays always made for rowdy passengers.

My job as a TSA screener wasn't glamorous, but it was necessary for our country. Sometimes it sucked to be the passengers' punching bag, but it paid the bills.

Beside me, two men walked briskly to the row of cars near mine. Those two had gotten off an international flight;

I'd watched them get off the plane in person, not over a security camera.

Their nationality was irrelevant to me, but the fact that each of them carried only a briefcase wasn't. I'd seen them step off the flight from Qatar. An international flight from Qatar was twenty-three hours, at best. Most of the time, layovers and delays put the trip closer to thirty hours. Traveling without luggage was a red flag. A big one.

We were trained to be aware of everything. I didn't want to be aware. I wanted to turn my brain off. My shift had ended, and I wanted to go home.

But it was too late. The men had my attention. After what happened to my brother…well, there wasn't much I wouldn't do to prevent that from happening to someone else.

If these men were terrorists, I wouldn't let them destroy another family.

With a sigh, I gave up on trying to talk myself out of it and followed the two men. This was way beyond the typical scope of work for me but I couldn't help myself.

A few miles from my cabin, they turned onto a side road, one clearly labeled for hauling supplies to a lumber camp. *Private Property*, it said.

There were no lights on the road, no buildings. I wasn't law enforcement and trespassing wasn't on my list of fun activities to do after dark.

If I called the police, these guys could turn out to be the owners of the lumber camp and then I'd look like a jackass, even though I'd had a reason.

I'd check the security footage tomorrow and find out where they entered customs. For now, I needed to get to my second job.

My little cabin was a welcome sight. It wasn't big, but it was cozy. The porch light glowed a warm amber and the snow sat perfectly atop the cedar log railing.

As soon as I'd bolted my front door, my phone rang. A photo of my parents at their fortieth anniversary party popped up. My watch said I had three minutes before I was on the clock for my second job.

"Hi, honey!" My mom's voice boomed over the phone line. "What are you doing?"

"Just walking in." My grimy uniform hit the floor; it could stay there for now. The hotline used voice-only calls instead of video, so I was going to wear pajamas for this shift.

"There's an opening here, at Portland International. You might even get a raise. Or a promotion!"

My mom never stopped campaigning to get me to move closer.

"I love you, mom, but I have to go." A clean pair of yoga pants made me feel a million times better. "Tell Lucy and dad I said hello."

"Oh," my mother's voice dropped. "That job. It's not…" she trailed off, but I knew what was coming. She asked me this question at least once a week. "It's not getting to you, right?"

The words she didn't say hung in the air. *I already lost your brother. I almost lost your sister. Why do you have to dwell on other people's suffering?*

"It's important. I'd do it full-time if it paid the bills." One day in the future, when I was a certified therapist, it would pay the bills.

"I'm sorry sweetheart," she said. "You know we don't want you to feel pressured to help us with the finances. We can manage just fine."

They couldn't manage, not even close, but there was no way I'd ever point that out. "I know mom. I want to."

After my brother died, my dad withdrew. My mom existed in a state of false cheeriness interspersed with extreme fretting. Neither of them were realistic about anything anymore. My practical, down-to-earth parents had disappeared forever. And my younger sister, Lucy, who'd been fifteen years old at the time, had coped with drugs and alcohol.

Finally off the phone, I got settled at my desk. The pajamas were comfy, but I couldn't lounge on the couch and forget that I was working. With a fresh cup of tea in hand, I logged in.

Within minutes, I had my first caller of the night. I took a deep breath. This evening shift had to be better than the shitty day I'd already endured.

NOAH

"*H*ello," a woman's voice said. "You've reached Crisis Counseling. I'm Adi. Can you tell me who you are?"

My back pressed against the bedroom wall until each vertebra dug into the plaster. Each breath stabbed through my chest. I pressed my hand over my face.

I couldn't even get my fucking name out.

"Take your time," she said.

For the first time since I got back, that kind of understanding comment didn't piss me off. If someone from my shifter clan expressed patience or sympathy, I couldn't stand it.

At least this woman was paid to pity me. I drew in one breath. Then another. I stared at the phone in my hand. "I'm Noah."

"Hi, Noah. It's nice to meet you. Can you tell me a little bit about why you're calling?" Her voice was low and her tone was even. Listening to her talk would be a much better option than talking about myself. Too bad that wasn't what we were doing here.

What the fuck was I going to say? *Someone betrayed me. Someone fucking betrayed me, our country, and our squadron. I lost my entire unit. Every single one. They weren't just my brothers in arms. They were my family—my clan—and the worst goddamn part is that one of them was the rat that sold us out.*

The rat had just been so damn stupid that he ended up getting blown away too.

I pushed my hands against my eyes as if the pressure would stop the images streaming across them. "Flashbacks."

"You're having flashbacks," she said. "Are those from recent combat?"

I pressed my spine harder against the sheetrock. "Yeah."

"How long ago?"

Taking a deep breath was impossible. It was no use. My breathing picked up until I was panting. Fuck. I hadn't been able to control my mind for weeks, but now I couldn't control my body either. "Three weeks."

"You haven't been home long."

Home. Right. I was home, instead of back in Pakistan, trying to figure out why our mission blew up and went straight to hell.

Home, in a dump of an apartment because I'd sold my own cabin when I thought I'd be on a year-long deployment.

I was home on administrative leave, which is the polite way of saying, *we don't fucking trust you with this anymore.* My shoulder blades dug into the plaster of the wall. "No. Not long."

Now on my feet, I walked to the other side of the room, then back. I'd walked ten-thousand steps in this room today. With each step, my chest got tighter.

Usually, when I was freaked out, I went out and shot something or I shifted into my bear form. Neither an option right now. My bear wanted out, but I couldn't leave the house. A soldier in the middle of a flashback was hard enough to cope with. A bear shifter in a flashback would be impossible.

"Noah, we don't have to talk about the flashbacks first," she said. "We can talk about other things."

"We can?" Part of me assumed this was being recorded by my commanding officer. Nothing would surprise me now. The counselor going off-script wasn't expected.

"Absolutely," she said. "Tell me about your favorite movie."

She had the sweetest voice. No way could she be a soldier. Not because she was female, but because she still had hope. She might know about trauma, but I'd bet she hadn't seen war, not up close. I was glad for that.

"It's uh...*Ghostbusters*."

"Yeah? I love that one too. Did you watch it as a kid?"

"Over and over." Growing up, my shifter clan wasn't big on television, but my aunt had a small one. Every time *Ghostbusters* came on, she'd yell for me to come over and she'd give me beef jerky from her secret stash to eat while I cheered on the good guys.

Becoming one of those good guys had been my goal ever since.

My chest wasn't being squeezed as hard. My breathing slowed. "That." I stopped walking and leaned my head against the wall. "That helped."

"I'm glad. If you're ready, we can go back to the reason you called now. Are you aware of anything in particular that brings them on? Some clients notice certain sounds, smells, or even phrases can cause flashbacks."

Yeah, I've noticed what brings them on. It's every fucking second I'm still alive and they aren't. How's that for a trigger? Having my commanding officer stonewall me from getting more info wasn't helping much either.

"They're pretty frequent right now." Frequent as in non-stop.

"Do you think you could start keeping track of what you're doing beforehand? Maybe try writing down what you're doing when one starts. Some survivors find that helpful."

I'd have to write down one word: living. That's what brought them on.

My throat burned. My vision tunneled. Nothing I did could stop this one from coming. My eyes closed against my will.

Some of my squad had been shifted when the attack happened. I'd been on sniper duty, so I'd been human that day. We were trained in every elite skill that humans use, including intelligence gathering, decoding, hand-to-hand combat, weapons, and surveillance, and on top of that, we were trained to fight as bears too.

Without warning, a blast threw me backward. Yellow light flashed over my eyes. Searing heat burned my face. I rolled behind a rock. Grit filled my mouth. Sand scraped against my cheek. My head spun. I pushed myself up but fell flat again.

Time passed in silence until sound began to flood back in. Screams. Roars. My squad was below me. I had to get to them. I flopped to my back and crawled, inch by inch, for twenty feet. Dust filled the air. Nothing was visible until I was right on top of my squad.

Dave's blue eyes were glassy. Blood dripped from his mouth. Josh's fur was a blur of red. No one moved. I crawled again, on my stomach, from shifter to shifter. No one was breathing.

My cousin lay on his side, not moving. "Chris!" My voice didn't work. "Chris," I croaked out. I shook him. "Come on." I pressed my head to his chest. No heartbeat.

Dust clogged my throat, but a tiny sound gave me hope. *Jesse.* Half-buried under rubble, ten feet away, his heart was still beating. "Jesse! Hang on. I'm coming."

"Noah?" A female voice called my name. "Noah!"

The underside of the bed was right in my face. To my right, the phone lay a few feet away on the shag carpet. Fun. I'd had a flashback and crammed myself under the bed...while I was on the phone. I pushed myself out, making the metal frame creak. It was a tight squeeze.

"I'm here," I stammered.

"Oh. I'm glad," she said. "Did you have one then?"

"Yeah. They don't stop."

"Okay. Don't give up, okay? There are so many options. I can get you connected to a counselor you can see in person. We can try medication. A lot of people are having luck with service dogs and therapy dogs."

Yeah, right. Meds didn't work on me, not unless there was an elephant tranq lying around. A dog would be nice until I turned into a bear and scared the piss out of it. Dogs are not a bear's best friend. A counselor might work if he or she was a shifter.

"This is good for now," I said. Her voice was soothing in a way nothing else had been.

"Yeah, that's great. You can call this hotline every day," she said. "You mentioned they're non-stop. Are you sleeping?"

"No." The nightmares were worse than the flashbacks.

"Do you want to tell me about what happens at night?"

Her voice calmed my jumbled nerves, but this was stupid. I couldn't tell her anything. Everything was classified.

And by the way, I've had to lock myself in my apartment because if I get really freaked out, I'm not going to harm myself, I'm going to turn into a bear.

I wasn't safe to be around. But unlike other headcases, a

taser couldn't take me out. Or a needle. Or even most gunshots.

How's that for a hotline call story she could tell her colleagues?

If I was lucky, she'd probably think I was having delusions.

I hung up.

ADELAIDE

"*N*oah?" I tapped my headset. "Noah, are you there?"

Nothing.

I checked the call log on the screen. He'd hung up.

My stomach twisted as I unplugged my headset. Hang-ups happened from time to time. All of the callers were dealing with a lot. Sometimes they got overwhelmed and they hung up. I wasn't allowed to call back, under any circumstances. If I felt like the caller was a threat to himself or others, I was supposed to contact my supervisor but I couldn't call back.

I hadn't wanted this one to hang up. His panic and misery came through loud and clear over the phone. I usually did a pretty good job of staying empathetic with the callers without letting them affect me personally. But this caller had been different. He'd affected me.

My thoughts lingered on him. I really hoped he would find some peace.

When I woke up the next day, Noah was still on my mind. I was scheduled to work the hotline again that night from seven to ten p.m. Maybe he'd call back during my shift, but for now, I had airport security to focus on.

Without clearance from my boss, I couldn't review the footage from last night.

"Do you have a minute?" I asked, sticking my head inside his office. It was stuffed full of discarded furniture and tangled cords. He waved me in, so I explained that I'd seen two guys leave last night from an international flight and they'd only had small briefcases.

"Where'd you say they came in from?"

"Qatar."

"And what'd they look like?"

"Medium height, medium build. Overall they were nondescript, but they did have on suits and they drove straight to a lumber site after dark." Inwardly I grimaced, hoping he wouldn't call me out for following them.

"Ethnically, were they Middle Eastern?"

"Yes," I said.

"Jeez." He smacked his forehead. "Why don't we just go ahead and write the headline?" He waved his hands above his head as if mimicking a banner in the air. "Are Passengers Having a Happy Thanksgiving in Maine where the Bangor Airport TSA Engages in Racial Profiling?"

Damn him. Following my training was the right thing to do. "You know that's not what's happening here. I'd have brought this to you if they were red-headed women from Finland."

He pointed at himself. "I know that." He pointed at me. "You know that." He dropped his arms. "No one else knows that. Nor do they care."

My hands went straight to my hips. "We need to do our jobs, without worrying about negative headlines."

"Tell that to the big boss then," he said. "Adelaide, we have an influx of people coming in today. We don't have time to investigate people who aren't even here, never mind discuss why you're taking your work home by following them. I'm doing to let that one go - for now." He made a shooing motion with his hands. "Get back to work. Screen the travelers that are here today. I'm sure they're just greedy businessmen trying to make a buck like the rest of us."

"Fine. I really hope that I'm an overly paranoid, suspicious freak who's spent too much time waiting for someone to do the worst." I leveled one last look at him. "I really do."

I caught the door with my arm before it slammed shut. Mateo was a decent boss when he wasn't worried about licking *his* boss' ass. He could be worse. A lot worse.

Back at my station, I did slam the nearest safety cone to the ground. Fine. If Mateo didn't care about criminals entering the country, I did.

Plenty of resources were available to me. I could quit and tell a reporter or I could go over his head. He was worried about the bad press if we investigated. Imagine the bad press if these two turned out to be evil? I guess he wouldn't mind a headline that said, "Bangor TSA Agents Ignore Security Threat and Cause Mass Destruction."

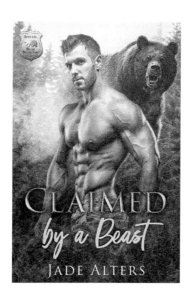

Click Here to Buy Now

XO, JADE

Reviews mean so much to indie authors like me. For years I struggled with doubts. Please consider reviewing this book if you enjoyed it. I'd appreciate it so much!

And if you haven't already, join my
exclusive readers list.

[Yes. Sign me up, please!]
Follow me on Facebook
JadeAlters.com

Visit my Publisher's Website
http://UntamedLoveRomance.com
for new releases weeks before their official release date!

The Spell's Price

Backfired Magic

Mated to the Pack

Taming Her Bears

Printed in Great Britain
by Amazon

15812319R00089